Conflict in Corinth & Memoirs of an Old Man

PAULIST PRESS ● *New York/Ramsey*

Conflict in Corinth & Memoirs of an Old Man

Two stories that illuminate the way
the bible came to be written

WALTER J. HOLLENWEGER

Copyright ©1978 by Chr. Kaiser Verlag, Munich. English translation
copyright ©1982 by Walter J. Hollenweger.

Library of Congress Catalog Card Number: 82-80165

ISBN: 0-8091-2455-6

Published by Paulist Press
545 Island Road, Ramsey, N.J. 07446

Printed and bound in the United States of America

CONTENTS

CONFLICT IN CORINTH

I AM A SECRETARY-SLAVE at the great Corinthian Bank of Trade and Commerce. We have branches in Patrae and Athens and also in Rome, Alexandria and Marseilles.[1] Our bank was founded about fifty years ago when the famous Isthmic Games were reintroduced.[2] We have a foreign exchange department for the many visitors who come to the great sports events and we also arrange credit for the heavy metal industry and occasionally for the provincial administration of Achaia.

One of my acquaintances is a secretary-slave with the provincial administration. His name is Tertius.[3] We met at the classes where we went to learn the Greek and Roman trade and commercial terms. For our work we both have to know not only the Greek but also the Roman trade language. It was Tertius who invited me to a religious service held by a sect called the Christians. I was interested in this sect which I knew only from hearsay, and I therefore took advantage of the opportunity of going with him. I would not have had the courage to go on my own.

One afternoon after the offices had closed, Tertius called for me at the bank. The last client had just left the building. I filed away the coins, letters of credit and books under the supervision of the head slave, and then Tertius and I set out together. "Today," he said, "we are having a particularly important meeting. The Corinthian Christians

3

sent a letter to the founder of our congregation, a man by the name of Paul, and today we intend to read and discuss part of his reply."

I knew something about this man Paul. Two or three years ago he had been involved in a quarrel with a particularly outspoken section of the Jewish synagogue. The affair had been brought before the pro-consul Gallio. He, however, soon realized that it was a private quarrel among the Jews relating to the interpretation of their books. He did not think it was his business to intervene, and in fact he looked on in a disinterested way when the chairman of their synagogue was beaten up.[4]

Most Corinthians thought that the sect of the Christians was part of the Jewish community. Others thought that their religion was pure superstition. For a time the Christians had met in the house of a certain Titus Justus who lived near the synagogue.[5] From comments made by our Jewish clients, however, it seemed clear to me—and my friend Tertius confirmed this—that the sect of the Christians had broken away from the synagogue after a violent row. The quarrel had centered on the question of circumcision, the sabbath and certain food taboos. The details did not interest me. Anyhow one has to be cautious when dealing with Jewish clients. Any unguarded questions about their religion might prompt them to take their business away from the Corinthian Bank of Trade and Commerce and transfer to the competition, the Graeco-Egyptian Credit Bank, and I could not afford to have any difficulties with my superior, the head slave. One should not forget that about a tenth of the inhabitants of Corinth are connected with the Jewish synagogue in some way or another.[6] So it is advisable to be cautious.

The Sect of the Christians
On this particular evening the meeting of the Christians did not take place in the house of Titus Justus. Tertius told

me that the Christian sect had grown to such an extent that they had to look for a larger place. That is why they now met in the house of the well-known Gaius.[7] He was a friend of Erastus,[8] the Chairman of the Department of Public Works in Corinth. Tertius worked under him, and I knew him as he was also a member of the board of directors of my bank. I also knew that the former chairman of the synagogue, Crispus,[9] another client of our bank (of course I am not at liberty to say anything on the nature of his dealings with our bank) was an important member of the Christian sect.

As we walked and talked I was suprised to hear Tertius always refer to the Christians as "the citizens' meeting of God." I had never before heard anybody use this old-fashioned expression (which I had only come across in history books) for a religious society. I asked him why they used such a strange expression as a name for their society. He did not know. "That is how we are called," he said, and added that he was quite sure that they were not just another religious society among the many in Corinth, but the new people of God, the latter-day saints, the citizenry of God. Well, well, I thought, like everybody else they do their best to sell themselves.

When we arrived at the house of Gaius there were already about twenty to thirty people there, mostly well-off people from Corinth, either secretary-slaves or house-slaves in middle-management positions like me or free upper middle class civil servants, and artisans. Of course Crispus, the former chairman of the synagogue, was there too, and Erastus, the Chairman of the Department of Public Works in Corinth. The latter greeted me with special attention which, I have to admit, flattered me. He said that he was happy to see me there and offered me some wine, grapes and nuts. On the whole there was a very relaxed atmosphere, very different from official receptions in Corinth. Each new arrival brought some fruit, bread, cheese, olives or flowers. Everything was put on a big table. I was a little embarrassed because I had not brought anything.

More and more people gathered in the courtyard. After dusk some dock workers also came along. I knew that they had arrived even before I saw them because of the typical smell of fish and salt water. After eight o'clock a clique of unskilled workers arrived—all of them slaves, as was obvious from their behavior—some of them from Upper Egypt and other distant parts of the Roman Empire. They did not speak Greek or Latin among themselves but some barbaric dialect. Erastus greeted them too and poured wine for them, just as he had for everybody else. But there was not sufficient wine to go around. They were obviously very thirsty!

Crispus and Gaius now stood behind a table on which there were a number of flat breads and a large cup. Opposite me, on the other side of the courtyard among the slaves and foreign workers, a somewhat exotic woman had attracted my attention. She had short dark hair and wore a purple gown. As far as I could see in the dim light of the torches which had now been lit, she played on a small hand drum, a kind of tambourine. The dock workers rose and beat time with their feet. They repeated one word over and over again in strong, syncopated rhythms, mixed with simple archaic harmonies. The word was "Marana-tha."[10] They emphasized the last two syllables: "Marana-tha." When they stopped singing and shouting, Crispus took one of the flat breads, held it up, and, after giving thanks to God, broke it and said: "This is my body, which is for you; do this in remembrance of me." I nudged Tertius because I thought that this was rather a bad joke. But to my astonishment his eyes were closed. He was praying and was unaware of what was happening around him.

The bread was broken into pieces and handed around. After a short while Crispus held up the cup and said: "This cup is the new covenant in my blood. When you drink it, do it in remembrance of me. For each time you eat this bread and drink the cup, you proclaim the death of the Lord, until he comes."[11]

Red Chloe Prophesies
The cup was passed around and the woman in the purple gown—I now learned that her name was Chloe[12]—played the hand-drum, and led by the foreign workers the Christians sang "Marana-tha, Marana-tha."

Chloe stood up and spoke violently and with closed eyes. She had covered her hair with a veil which glowed red in the light of the torches. She looked to me like an oracle priestess of ancient Greece. I did not understand what she was saying. It sounded to me as if she were speaking in a foreign tongue for the foreign workers.

But when she had stopped speaking, one of the foreigners spoke in broken, but clearly understandable, Greek. It was obvious that he was interpreting Chloe. As far as I can remember he said, "Before me, all are equal, Jew and Greek, slave and freeman, man and woman. Honor him or her as a saint of God. In God's people there are only saints; nobody is more saintly than anybody else! Thus speaks the Lord."

As soon as the interpretation was over a general discussion broke out. The foreigners and slaves who were gathered on the opposite side of the court gesticulated and sometimes shouted something over to our side, but I could not make out what they were saying. I could only understand those who were standing next to me. These were a group of more affluent Christians. They said, "We wonder how long Crispus and Gaius will put up with the noise of Chloe's people. Do we have to listen Sunday after Sunday to this hoi polloi? Not to speak of the fact that their understanding of the Christian faith is a bit too rudimentary. It is true they do not expect that the Christians will

7

deliver them from slavery in society, but they want to be treated as equals in the worship service—that seems pretty clear from their behavior. Sometimes one gets the impression that they are even proud of their spiritual and material misery."

I watched Erastus leave the court of the villa and saw him return carrying a scroll under his arm. As he had greeted me so warmly at the beginning of the meeting, I was encouraged to ask him what this was all about. "Well, you see," he said, "Christians are basically different from other religious societies in Corinth. The Christians do not hold separate religious services for slaves and freemen, which would make it awkward for the better educated slaves who would not know to which group they really belonged." He mentioned this on purpose as he knew that I was one of these. I asked, "But does this mixture of cultures and social status not create a number of financial and psychological problems?" "It certainly does," he replied, "as you can see for yourself in this meeting. And what you have heard is not the only controversy in the Christian community. You surely know that I as Chairman of the Department of Public Works in Corinth[13] have to attend many banquets and receptions, festivities where the meat which is served comes from the temples here in Corinth, and which has been offered ceremonially to idols.[14] You are certainly aware that I would have to resign from my job if I did not take part in these banquets. However, I am of the opinion that for a Christian everything is allowed, including attending business banquets and political dinners where we prepare important contracts and political compromises."

Tertius interrupted Erastus. "It is not only the meat which has been offered to the idols that Chloe protests about. She says she knows that the Corinthian courtesans go to these banquets—business and political courtesans."

"Prostitutes who are used to win certain contracts you

8

mean?" I asked. From my work in the bank I knew that such things went on.

"No comment," Erastus said. He added, "One is expected to drink a toast with these courtesans but otherwise one has no further obligations." The topic was obviously embarrassing for him, but he mentioned in passing, "You must not take too seriously the criticisms which Chloe throws at us. This somewhat exalted women's lib apostle has no family to help her feel important and wanted, only her followers, the foreign dock workers and slaves, to boost her ego."

This was obviously a sign to end the conversation. Erastus now went forward with the scroll and rolled it out. A Christian stood on either side of him holding a torch. Gaius introduced him. "Just as Paul wrote a letter to the Romans while he was here in Corinth—you surely remember how he worked day and night—so he has written a long reply to us from Ephesus. For many Sundays we have already read parts of his reply, and we come today, so it seems to me, to one of the most important and instructive passages. Please read, Erastus."

The Meeting of God's Citizens
The two torch-bearers drew nearer to Erastus and there was absolute silence in the courtyard. Erastus began, "For Christ is like a single body with its many limbs and organs, which, many as they are, together make up one body. For indeed we were all brought into the one body by baptism in the one Spirit, whether we are Jews"—and here he looked at Crispus—"or Greeks"—he stopped as if he wanted to say, "As I am"—"whether slaves"—and when he uttered this word Chloe's people and the dock workers threw their hands in the air and shouted in a mighty chorus, "Halleluja, Kyrios Jesous!" Then the shout took the form of a fugue or a hymn. "Halle-, halle-, halleluja! Jesus is Lord! Halle-, halle-, halleluja! Jesus is Lord!" And

9

finally everybody, not only the slaves, joined in the shout, "Jesus is Lord!"

"You are right," Erastus continued, "but listen to how he goes on: whether slaves or free men"—and now there was a hush, for the Christians born as free men or those who had been given freedom by their slavemasters stood in superior silence—"we have been immersed into one Holy Spirit."[15] "Amen, halleluja," the meeting responded.

But now Chloe stood up again. "And the women—has he forgotten the women?"

Erastus looked at his manuscript. "I do not find that he mentions the women."

Another woman, Phoebe from the port of Cenchreae,[16] rose to her feet. She spoke softly and slowly. "It is not necessary to mention women. We are here. We take part in the service. We are immersed into one Holy Spirit. Nobody can deny that." Some of the men around me sighed deeply. But they did not speak.

Erastus continued, "A body is not one single organ, but many. Suppose the foot should say, 'Because I am not a hand, I do not belong to the body,' it belongs to the body nonetheless. Suppose the ear were to say, 'Because I am not an eye, I do not belong to the body,' it still belongs to the body. If the body were all eye, how could it hear? If the body were all ear, how could it smell? But, in fact, God appointed each limb and organ to its own place in the body as he chose. If each organ had the same function, how could the body function as a whole? That is why there are many different organs, but one body."[17]

During these somewhat difficult sentences I noticed that the dock workers and the slaves on the left-hand side of the court had let their attention wander. I wondered whether they knew enough Greek to follow this reading. Some of them began to walk around and to look on the tables for something to eat. They found a few grapes and were content to sit in a corner and eat them. On the other side of the court attention grew. Some nodded their heads in agreement or murmured softly, "Yes, that's right!" Titus Justus, whom I recognized by his Jewish prayer bands, whispered something. He said, "Too many philosophical quotations, Livius and Plato."[18] "Well, do not forget, he also quotes Josephus, the Jewish writer," his neighbor whispered in reply.

Erastus Criticized

Erastus continued, "The eye cannot say to the hand, 'I do not need you,' nor the head to the feet, 'I do not need you.' Quite the contrary: those organs of the body which seem to be weaker than others are indispensable"—and here I noted how one of the dock workers stopped chewing and spat out the grape which he had just put into his mouth— "and those which we regard as less honorable are treated with special honor. To our unseemly parts is given a more than ordinary respect. The respectable parts do not need it.'"[18]

"Amen," shouted the slave who had just spat out the grape. "If that be true then Erastus had better give the money he donated toward the paving of the main street in Corinth[20] to us, the slaves, for the respectable ones do not need it, but we, the weaker ones, we could make good use of it."

Erastus stopped. It hurt him that his political life, in which, as he had told me, compromises were necessary, was discussed in church. He did not defend himself, but asked Gaius to take over the chairmanship of the meeting. "No, not Gaius," the same slave shouted. "Why could it not be one of us for a change?"

"Very well," Gaius replied. "Which of you can read, for we want to continue our reading of Paul's letter?" It turned out that none of the dock workers or slaves could read. Only Phoebe from Cenchreae, in whom they obviously had confidence, and we the better-educated slaves could read. That is how my friend Tertius came to be asked to continue the reading. I could see that he trembled nervously when they chose him. But he went forward, and when he took the scroll from Gaius' hands everyone applauded.

He asked to be shown the passage where the reading should continue. At first he read with hesitation, but the more he read the clearer and more distinct his voice became. His face shone in the awareness that he could communicate something important and helpful. He read, "But *God*"—and he emphasized the word "God"—"but *God* has put the various parts of the body together, giving special honor to the humbler parts, so that there might be no split in the body and that all the parts might care for each other."[21]

When he said this, Erastus went to the slave who had interrupted him, sat next to him on the floor and engaged in a long conversation which of course I could not hear.

Tertius continued, "If one organ suffers, they all suffer together. If one flourishes, they all rejoice together. Now you are Christ's body and each of you a limb or organ of it."[22]

Tertius rolled up the scroll. The community sang a Jewish psalm, in Greek translation of course. They stood together for a while and talked. I asked Tertius for permission to copy the passage which had been read to us. While I was writing I felt somebody's eyes on me. When I turned around I discovered Chloe.

"You are right to copy this passage of our apostle Paul. His letters are tremendous. When he was with us he was not much of a public speaker. But his letters, they get right under the skin."[23] I realized that she could read, for she followed my writing with her eyes. "You are astonished," she continued, "that a woman who is generally seen in the company of slaves and dock workers can read. I would have liked to read publicly when Tertius was asked to continue the reading. But that would have stirred up even more hostility against what some call the 'women's regiment.' That is why I kept quiet."

I stood up and looked at the woman. Something about her appeared to me to be both familiar and strange. Where had I met that perfume, that hair style, that eye-shadow? I asked myself. Then it dawned on me. Her appearance bore a striking resemblance to the courtesans who enhanced the symposia of the directors of our bank. I did not want to mention this, for a courtesan at a Christian religious meeting—that was a little out of place, it seemed to me.

She seemed to guess my thoughts and said, "Yes, sir, I was a courtesan, or, if you prefer, a well-educated and well-paid prostitute, whom the businessmen of Corinth used to influence their clients. That is what I *was*. Then I became a Christian and gave up my 'profession.' This body of prostitution has become a temple of the Holy Spirit." "How then do you now earn your living?" I asked, somewhat too curiously perhaps. "I keep a local inn for dock workers and slaves. That way I can just make a living."

I did not want to ask further questions and so I took my leave.

Why They Became Christians
On the way home Tertius and I walked a long time side by side in silence. Finally I said, "I understand a little why you Christians call yourselves the 'citizens' meeting of God' and not something like 'religious cultic association' or 'assembly of the Christians' or even 'Christian synagogue.'[24] Indeed what you do is totally different from what other religious societies in Corinth do, where like meets like. In the Christian meeting, cultures, languages, social status, men and women, Jews and Greeks, meet in one and the same place. And in spite of these enormous differences it seems that there is something like a belonging together even if sometimes the antagonisms seem to be stronger

13

than the fellowship."

"Can you explain to me," I now asked Tertius, "why Gaius and Erastus have become Christians?"

"You will understand that better when you have come to more meetings," he answered. "The short answer is, however, that they have found salvation, a center of life, a task and a hope. Perhaps I should explain that both Erastus and Gaius participated in the worship of the Jewish synagogue for a long time. But they never could become full members. You know that Jews make circumcision compulsory. And when they go to the fitness training in the great gymnastics hall in Corinth where the men of the upper-class meet regularly, Jewishness cannot be hidden. On top of this Jews have certain rules concerning the sabbath and food. How then could a Jew be the Chairman of the Department of Public Works? The Christians, on the other hand, provided Erastus with the opportunity of adopting all that made sense to him in Judaism—the one God, the ethics, a sense of meaning—without cutting himself off from public life in Corinth."

"And the slaves?" I asked further. "Well, the slaves," he said, "many of them have been invited by Red Chloe. She has a magical power over them. The slaves hardly ever meet a lady of her beauty, culture and inner spiritual strength who talks with them, the uneducated and uncultured slaves. She invites them to the citizens' meeting of the Christians and talks to them about the Lord of the Christians, Lord of the slaves and free men. When they come they experience these meetings of God's citizens as a place where they are taken seriously with all their gifts."

"What does it mean to be immersed in the Holy Spirit?" I continued. "To be immersed in one Spirit," he replied, "is a reference to baptism. If you would like to, you can meet me again next Sunday. But this time it will be at three o'clock in the morning. We are having a baptismal

14

service at a river. Then you can see for yourself what it means to be immersed in one Spirit. We Christians believe that the Holy Spirit, the Spirit of God, takes possession of human beings at baptism, purifies them, and all that is good in them, for the service of God and man, and controls that which is evil in them."

"And you," I finally asked when we arrived at the doorstep of his lodging, "why are you a Christian?"

"I was invited by my superior, Erastus (who is also my slave master), to go to a meeting of the Christians. Since getting to know the Christians, I have learned how to deal with that great anger inside me, an anger which you must know too, which is rooted in the fact that we secretary-slaves are not taken seriously by the common working slaves or by the free artisans and businessmen. Have you never experienced that anger, a feeling of angry help-lessness because we are always in-between?"

"Of course I have," I replied, "but what has that to do with Christian faith?" The words were hardly out of my mouth when I realized that my question had already been answered. I would never forget how Tertius looked as he read the important sentences in Paul's letter while the flickering torches on either side of him lit up his radiant face.

Finally he said, "This is what it has to do with faith—that I as a secretary-slave in the Department of Public Works in Corinth can be a voice, a tool of God."

Baptism at Dawn
On the following Sunday morning Tertius awakened me at three o'clock in the morning. A full hour's walk lay ahead of us, but I looked forward to hearing more from Tertius about "being immersed in the Spirit," an experience which the Christians call baptism.

We set off. As it was still dark we took oil lamps with us. Here and there a dog barked as we passed by the closed

15

doors. We left the city and walked up through an olive grove. When we arrived at the top of the hill we were able to blow out our lamps as the stars had begun to fade. We sat down and I played with a stick in the soft earth. Between the longish leaves of the olive trees one could visualize the sea rather than see it.

"Tell me, Tertius," I asked—"that which the Christians call baptism, is it not something which the Jews know too? Some of the Corinthians who became Jews were submitted to a kind of water-experience, which they call baptism."

"That's right," Tertius replied, "but the ceremony and the significance of the Jewish baptism is different from ours."

"Is it then similar to the sacraments of the mystery religions? I know that the disciples of the Dionysian mystery religions undergo certain ceremonies vicariously for their forebears."[85]

Tertius did not like the parallel. But he replied patiently, "Certainly Christians too know baptism for the dead, but you will see for yourself that the Christian baptism is not like any other religious ceremony. Baptism unites Christians in one body. This is probably similar to the Jewish and mystery religions. Christian baptism creates a communion between Christians and between Christians and their Lord. This is different from the Jewish and mystery religions. This Lord Christ is in fact present at the baptismal service."

"Is he the one of whom it was said last Sunday that he died for us?" I asked.

"Yes," he replied, "he is the same. He is the first and so far the only one who has overcome death and who therefore is now not only the Lord of the Christians but the Lord of the whole world." I looked at him bemused and surprised. Up to now I had considered Tertius to be a reasonable man. But that he could seriously state that his Christ had died but nevertheless is present at the baptismal

16

service—this I could not understand.

However, many remarkable things happen in Greece, especially in the field of religion. It is said of several miracle workers that they have risen from the dead. But as to how Tertius could say that the founder of the insignificant sect of the Christians was the Lord of the world, that was indeed an enigma to me. All the world knows that the Caesar in Rome is the lord of the world. Of course we Greeks do not like this, and our defeat at the hands of the Romans is also the reason why I, as a non-Roman, am only a secretaryslave and not, like the Roman civil servants of my rank and education, a highly paid and respected under-secretary to the pro-consul. But I did not ask further questions and so we walked on.

We now left the path and descended into a gorge. We could hear the river roaring, and soon we came upon a basin which the river had carved out in the rock over the centuries. It seemed as if the water turned around in a circle, partly flowing underneath the rock. On our side of the river the water was foaming white. Where it flowed underneath the rock it looked olive green. About thirty to forty Christians stood at the water's edge facing the rock. Tertius and I remained at a respectful distance because he was not sure whether or not the Christians, and in particular the baptismal candidates, would perhaps be embarrassed by the presence of an outsider. As the service took place in the open air, they could not altogether avoid being seen by passers-by. However, as Tertius explained, there was nothing secret about baptism.

I saw that Red Chloe was also there with some of her people. I also noticed Crispus, the former chairman of the synagogue. On the other hand I could not see Erastus, the Chairman of the Department of Public Works of Corinth. Gaius stayed somewhere in the background. Chloe's people sang a beautiful morning hymn:

17

"Awake, sleeper,
Rise from the dead,
And Christ will shine upon you."[86]

They sang it several times, and with each stanza they added new harmonies. Then one of the slaves walked into the water—"His name is Fortunatus,"[27] Tertius whispered to me—and prayed a kind of water- or consecration-prayer which, however, I could not understand. Suddenly there was a total silence. I heard only the steady roaring of the water punctuated by the occasional song of a bird. When the sun sent her first rays down through the olive grove and they slanted into the basin, all the Christians began to sing the hymn which I had first heard at the meeting in Gaius' villa: "Halle-, halle-, halleluja. Jesus is Lord. Halle-, halle-, halleluja. Jesus is Lord!" The two baptismal candidates threw off their clothes and were led by a slave to Fortunatus. He cried aloud, "Jason, I baptize you in the name of Jesus. Amen." He immersed him in the river and the Christians shouted, "Amen!"

Immediately following he dipped the second slave under the water and cried, "Quartus, I baptize you in the name of Jesus. Amen."[28] "Amen," the Christians shouted again. The two were led back to the shore, wrapped in white gowns and rubbed until they were dry. While Fortunatus was rubbing them he said to them, "Baptized into union with him, you have all put on Christ as a gown."[29]

The Christians left singing. I had remarked that Fortunatus had baptized the two "in the name of Jesus," but later had told them that they were baptized "into union with Christ." I asked Tertius what that meant. He did not know. "We have always done it this way," he told me.

However, he knew that some said, "Anathema Jesous,[30] accursed by *Jesus the Jew*. Our Savior is the *risen Christ*," while others, who claimed to follow Paul, believed that the risen Christ was none other than Jesus the Jew. It was obvious that these religious differences reflected existing class differences—as I had already observed on the previous Sunday. Obviously those who could read Paul's letters, that is, the better-educated and well-off Christians, stood more on the side of Paul. Earlier in their lives each of them had been associate members of the synagogue. The Jewish tradition, which they learned from the great Greek translation of the Septuagint, and the stories of the Jew, Jesus of Nazareth, were for them a necessary part of the Christian faith.

The dock workers and slaves, however, called "Red Chloe's people" for short, who had never been part of the synagogal community and who could not read and who therefore had no knowledge of the Jewish tradition—these people relied rather on their spontaneous inspiration which they then related to the risen Christ. In this matter they were much more gifted than Crispus, Gaius, Erastus, Stephanas and the other influential and affluent Christians in Corinth.

In spite of this explanation it was not clear to me how Tertius could maintain that this Lord Christ was present at the baptismal service. I certainly had not seen him, unless the risen Lord of the Christians was one and same as the rising sun which had bathed the whole scene in its dazzling morning light. I asked Tertius once again whether or not this Christ had been present at the baptismal service.

"Yes, he was there," he said without hesitation. "Did you not realize it?"

I had not realized it.

The Inn of the "Christians for Socialism"

Red Chloe had an inn near the baptismal pool. It was known locally as "Koinonia Christianon" which one could perhaps freely translate as "The Inn of the Christians for Socialism." That is where we were invited to take breakfast.

It was a festive and happy meal. We were offered fruit, wine, bread and grilled fish. I enjoyed it.

When everybody was well fed, Crispus stood in front of the people and announced that Erastus was going to read a further passage from Paul's letter. Erastus had not taken part in the baptismal service and had only arrived in time for the breakfast.

Chloe protested loudly and firmly. "No," she said. "We are here in my house. Why should we always listen to Paul's letters? If he came himself, that would be quite different. Then we could experience healings, miracles and visions. But his letters are too difficult for our people, and on top of this they are biased. On what authority does he guide us from Ephesus? We too have received the Holy Spirit, who leads us in all truth. What do we need the written directions of Sir Rabbi Paul for?"

Everyone was taken aback. To my astonishment Tertius, my friend, spoke up. "Whether Paul has anything to say to us or not, that we can only judge when we have read his letter. Remember, dear Chloe, that you owe it to the endurance, the courage and the inner strength of Paul that you have found the way from darkness to light. We all are in his debt."

"No," said Erastus. "Paul himself says that we owe it to Christ."

"Amen. Halleluja," Chloe's people shouted again in wild tumult.

"We owe it to Christ," Erastus continued when the noise had died down, "that we found the way from darkness to light. But this Christ refers us to the brothers, including to brother Paul. That is why I am now going to continue to read from his letter."

He began: "I may speak in tongues of men or of angels, but if I am without love, I am like a circus gong or a hand-drum."[31]

The better-off slaves and the more influential

Christians began to smile, and this smile gradually broke into laughter. Chloe in her red gown blushed all over her face. It was she who led the Christians in the singing with her hand-drum and who had spoken in tongues on the previous Sunday. For once she was at a loss and remained silent. I felt sorry for her.

Erastus continued, "I may have the insights of the Jewish prophets, the astute knowledge of Greek scientists and all spiritual wisdom, I may have faith strong enough to move mountains; but if I have no love, I am nothing."[32]

Erastus stopped. Chloe was recovering from her shock. She looked up again. The slaves, without saying anything, looked at Erastus, Tertius, Gaius, Stephanas and the other educated Christians, who lowered their heads and remained silent.

It is clear, I thought to myself, that what matters to these Christians is neither religious enthusiasm—expressed in speaking in tongues—nor theological and practical knowledge. What counts for them is only what one does, living for others, a life of practical love. Erastus continued, "And I may spend all I possess in order to feed the dock workers, the poor slaves and the foreign workers, and I may burn my body in a public place in protest against an unjust order of society; but if I have no love, I am none the better."[33]

The sentence confused me. The actions of practical love are not what Paul understands by love. "What does he mean by love?" I wanted to ask Tertius. But Erastus continued:

"Love is patient.
Love is kind and not excitable.
Love is not boastful.
Love is not puffed up.
Love is not snobbish.
Love is not selfish.

21

It is not quick to take offense.
Love keeps no score of wrongs.
Love does not enjoy injustice
but rejoices with truth.
There is nothing that love cannot face.
It endures all things, believes all things, hopes all
things."[34]

Erastus paused again. Nobody spoke a word. I wanted to make a comment, and as Erastus looked in my direction, I took my courage in my hands and said, "What Paul understands by love is something which is quite well-known in Greece. It is the balance of soul and mind.[35] The whole passage—and I wonder what this means to you—argues without ever mentioning your Christ. It is identical to what philosophers and gentlemen teach us: an educated man is unduly affected neither by joy nor by sadness. Success and failure leave him unmoved. But I must hasten to add that what I have seen so far among you does not add up to this Greek ideal. You are normal people who do not suppress their anger, their antipathy and sympathy even if this behavior of yours is in contradiction to Paul's writings. And I must say that this normal approach does not strike an outsider in an unsympathetic way—on the contrary."

Erastus looked at me as if he wanted to say, "You are right, but why did you have to say it?"

"No, no, no," Chloe said firmly, but not as loudly as she usually spoke. "No, Paul has always disagreed with the sophistication and objective wisdom of the Greeks. He was himself a man of explosive temperament. If he had been just another Greek philosopher, teaching us a general kind of loving humanity and objectivity, then there wouldn't be any Christians in Corinth. There must be another explanation."

That made sense to me. "Perhaps the explanation lies in the rest of the letter. Please, go on reading," Gaius said.

And Erastus continued,

> "Love will never come to an end.
> Prophetic insights will cease.
> Speaking in tongues, religious ecstasy will vanish.
> Religious and scientific knowledge will pass away,
> for our knowledge is provisional,
> our religious insights are provisional, partial,
>   fragmentary.
> But when that which is perfect is come
> the provisional and fragmentary will come to an
>   end."[36]

I did not understand a thing. What did the Christians mean by "the perfect" which shall come? I had no time to think because Erastus continued:

"When I was a child, my speech, my outlook, and my thoughts were all childish. When I grew up, I had finished with childish things. Now we see only puzzling reflections in a mirror, but then we shall see face to face. My knowledge now is provisional and fragmentary; then I shall know as I am known."[37]

"Paul concludes this passage," Erastus said, "with the hymn which all of us know—'And now abideth....'"

The Christians joined in the hymn which transformed Red Chloe's humble inn "Kononia Christianon" into a beautiful temple.

"And now abideth faith," some sang. Others added, "And now abideth hope." And a third group joined in singing, "And now abideth love." And all three groups sang together the final stanza, "But the greatest of these is love."[38]

The Vision
There was a silence. I felt restless because I had to be at work by nine o'clock. But then Red Chloe stood up and

23

spoke with closed eyes,

> "Behold, I see an enormous trombone
> which reaches over the whole of the Aegean Sea.
> Its bell-mouth opens above
> the city of Corinth,
> and a sound goes out.
> It is the first of the last sounds.
> And the sound sweeps the ships from the sea.
> And the businessmen and bankers,
> the publicans and temple priests,
> heathens and Christians,
> Jews and Greeks,
> throw aside their tools and pens,
> their books and holy vessels,
> and fall on their faces,
> for the perfect has come,
> vanished is the fragmentary.
> He comes on the clouds of the sky.
> Marana-tha."

The whole congregation joined in the hymn "Marana-tha."

It was now time for Tertius and me to return to Corinth. I found the vision of the big trombone confusing. The baptismal service had great appeal for me. I found Red Chloe's inn genuine and authentic. But the vision—no, thank you. I shared my reservations with Tertius.

"The vision," he said, "is an image of hope. We Christians have a hope. The hope is that our Lord Christ will come again. And then God's justice will be revealed, and all people will recognize him as their Lord."

"I don't understand a thing," I commented. "You told me that your Lord Christ has died for all people. Then you said that he was present at the baptismal service. And now you say that, although he is already here, he will come again. Is he then not already here?"

"How can I explain that to you?" Tertius tried again.

"This Christ is here, but invisibly, that is to say, not totally invisibly. He is visible in the life of Chloe and her people, in her inn. He is visible in the life of Erastus and—I hope—also in my life. But this is a very puzzling, fragmented vision. We cannot point to the meeting of the Christians, we cannot point to baptism and say, 'Look, here he is.' We cannot point to the lives of the Christians and say, 'Look, here he is.' But when the perfect is come, that is to say, when he comes himself visibly, then the provisional and fragmentary vision will be swallowed up in the perfect vision. What we live here provisionally is something like a preface, a prelude to the main theme. But the premiere of the concert is still ahead."

"If that be the case, then is your actual concrete life not very important?" I wanted to know.

He replied, "It is important in the sense in which a prelude is important. We must play in the right tonality. It is important in the sense of a herald who announces the king's arrival. We are not the main performance. We are not the king. But when he comes—and that will be very soon—we can disappear from the scene."

"Are you sure that he will come soon?" I asked.

"Very sure," he said confidently. "That is why we sing in all our services 'Marana-tha, Lord, come soon!' And he comes."

During the following week something else came. There were riots on the docks. Some of the dock workers had complained that they did not have enough to eat. The foreign workers in particular said that they lacked the strength to tackle the heavy work because they did not have their usual onion, pepper and garlic sauce. The Greek spices, they said, were much too weak. One of their leaders was put in prison and lashed. In retaliation three dock workers beat up one of the supervisors. That was the signal for the port authorities to put some of the loudest agitators in prison and to charge them with malicious conspiracy against the public interest. That was quite a serious matter because capital punishment was a definite possibility in such cases. I also had heard that the two Christians who had been baptized that very Sunday, Quartus and Jason, were involved in the matter. I wanted to know how Christians would react to this situation and decided to go to their next meeting.

Women, Be Quiet!

I arrived late at Gaius' house the following Sunday. Because of the riots in the port and the risk that some of the ships might be set on fire, we had to complete some urgent insurance transactions. I could not leave the bank at the usual time and arrived only about half past seven.

When I entered his villa I heard strange singing. It seemed as if the whole citizens' meeting of the Christians was singing in ten or twenty parts. I could not understand the words, but I soon realized that this must be the singing in tongues which I had heard mentioned several times in Paul's writings. Although everyone sang his own melody so to speak, the harmonies fitted together. It was as if the Christians were building a temple of sounds, a social acoustic sanctuary under whose roof they could feel at home.

Unlike my first visit I was not able to sit with my friend Tertius. He told me that it was customary for newcomers, the non-initiated, to be seated in special places, on benches at the back and down the sides. These benches were called "Idiots'-Seats"[39] because those sitting on them were considered by the Christians to be uninformed, uninitiated, *idiotai*. Sitting on one of these seats I was able to follow the service very well.

The distribution of wine and bread followed the pattern of the previous Sundays. I do not need to repeat this. But when Erastus, the Chairman of the Department of

Public Works in Corinth, went forward with the scroll from which he intended to read and when the two torch-bearers took their positions at either side of him, Chloe—who else?—rose to her feet and protested.

"With respect, brothers and sisters," she said, "how can you just carry on with the reading from the learned texts of our brother Paul after all that has happened in our city during this week? Do you not know that Jason, whom we baptized last Sunday in the name of Jesus, and who had been baptized with us together into one body, as Paul says—this same Jason is in prison? Does Paul not say that if one organ or limb suffers, all suffer? And Jason suffers. Do we not suffer with him? Do you know that he has been unjustly accused of rioting? It is surely clear to the gentlemen and brothers from the city administration here present"—and she looked at Gaius and Erastus, but glanced also briefly at Tertius—"that if the accusation can be upheld in court, his crucifixion is inevitable. Two weeks ago Tertius read from Paul's letter, 'God has put the various parts of the body together, giving special honor to the humbler parts, so that there might be no split in the body and that all the parts might care for each other.'[40] Jason[41] is in serious trouble. Do we not care about him?"

Some of the slaves and dock workers, who had gathered as usual on the left-hand side of the inner-court of the villa around Red Chloe, stood up. Erastus held up his hand as if he wanted to say something, but Gaius began to speak and said somewhat brusquely to Chloe, "Sister Chloe, Paul does not favor women talking publicly in the citizens' meeting of the Christians."[42]

"That is your invention, brother Gaius," she protested.

"No," Erastus replied, "here it is written: Women should not address the meeting. They have no license to speak, but should keep their places as the law directs. If there is something they want to know, they can ask their own husbands at home. It is a shocking thing that a woman should address the congregation."

Chloe was silent for a moment. Then she took courage and said, "You would like that Gaius, wouldn't you? You want to reintroduce the Jewish law. But this law was abolished by Christ. And what husband should I ask at home?" Some laughed, as they knew that she was not married. "Anyhow," she continued, "may I see the passage?"

Chloe went up to the table and was shown the scroll. "That is in another handwriting," she commented, "and furthermore these sentences are written on a different piece of parchment which has been stuck on later.[43] I do not believe that this was written by Paul. This is contradicted by other things he writes. Have we women not received the Holy Spirit just as you men have?"

The slaves, both men and women on the left-hand side of the meeting, broke out in a wild uproar. "Praise the Lord. Yes, amen." Only Phoebe from Cenchreae remained silent.

"And," Chloe continued, "has Paul not said that women should wear a veil when prophesying? That is why I bought this red veil." And then she concluded in a soft voice, "I would prefer to remain silent if one of you gentlemen would take up the cause of the accused slaves. Do you not remember what happened last year? Among those crucified who were exposed in a long row of crosses at the port, there was a Christian. The leaders of the riot had heaped all the blame on him and tried to capitalize on the general suspicion and contempt for the Christians."

Living with Conflicts
Chloe sat down. Meanwhile Gaius had listened with great attention.

"Chloe is right," he said. "We must send a delegation to the pro-consul. And it seems to me that you, Erastus, should lead that delegation. We have to inform the pro-consul that we consider that to convict Christians of rioting is politically unwise and unjust and that we would not hesitate to appeal to Rome against the ruling of the courts in Corinth in order to stop what we consider this miscarriage of justice. True, 'love endures all things, believes all things, hopes all things.'[44] But that does not mean that we accept without comment criminal breach of justice. Paul also says that 'love does not enjoy injustice but rejoices with truth.' "[45]

I thought to myself: But suppose Christians were accused of undermining society because the very form of their worship service questions existing law and order? Would it not be a just accusation, because in their services foreigners, slaves and women are considered equal—or almost equal. This could be seen as a kind of spiritual revolution. Their belief in a coming kingdom of God which will be inaugurated by the last trumpet surely relativizes and questions the existing holy Roman Empire. Nobody in his right mind can question these facts. It is possible that Jason is justly accused according to Roman law. And if he is crucified according to the law, what will Erastus, Gaius and Chloe do then? I could not answer my question.

In the meantime the excitement had died down. Red Chloe and her people seemed to agree to Gaius' proposal. The torch-bearers approached Erastus and he began to read again.

"If I pray in tongues, my spirit prays but my mind remains barren. What then? I will sing with the spirit, and I will sing with the mind. To sing with the spirit," Erastus looked up from his manuscript and added, "refers to that which we did at the beginning of our meeting when all sang together in tongues in many harmonies. To sing with the mind refers to that which we did last Sunday, when we sang the hymn which we all know, 'And yet abideth....' According to Paul both have their place in the service. I continue: If you sing with the Spirit how shall the one who is sitting on the seat of the idiot, the uninitiated"—and all looked over to me—"how shall he understand what you pray? You may go through a wonderful religious experience but it is of no help to the other man."[46]

"We do not sing and pray for the others," said Quartus, one of the two slaves who had been baptized the previous Sunday. He had been taken into custody on a charge of alleged rioting and he had been scourged, but then released with a warning to mend his ways. "We sing and pray for us," he said. "There are certain things which we have to do for our own benefit as almost everything that we do is for others—for instance, being punished and scourged for others." His hand touched his back and his face looked half-comical, half-sad. "Always carrying bags for the rich people, always working for others. At least in the worship service we would like to do something for ourselves. There we sing for us, and speak in tongues for us."

"Amen, amen," shouted the slaves on the left-hand side of the gathering.

Erastus continued, "Paul is not against speaking in tongues. The next sentence shows this very clearly. He writes: 'Thank God, I speak more in tongues than all of you, but in the congregation I would rather speak five intelligible words for the benefit of others as well as myself, than thousands of words in tongues. Do not be childish, my friends. Be as innocent of evil as babes, but at least be grown up in your thinking.' "[47]

"Paul is unjust and he does not understand us," Quartus interrupted again. "Certainly, we should be grown up in our thinking. But we do not think as the scribes like Erastus, Gaius, Tertius and Paul think. We are Christians without books. You think with a pen in your hand. You think in sentences and arguments. We think in images and visions.[48] We think with the whole body, not just with the head. Do you really think that my back does not think when the whip is dancing on it, or when I carry the heavy bags on the docks? Because we think with the whole of our bodies, speaking in tongues helps us to grow up in thinking. Why can't you ever understand this? We can't afford the luxury of limiting thinking to reading and writing. It is bad enough that for ten weeks already we have had to listen to Paul's letter."

"Do you not want to hear the rest of the letter?" Erastus asked.

"Sure we want to hear it," Quartus replied. "We want to know what Paul has to say. But we shall always protest when we disagree."

"That is right," Erastus said. "That is part of the body, part of thinking in the body, as you say, that conflicts are not suppressed. However, Paul is concerned not only with Christians but with the world as a whole. He thinks that our service must make a newcomer so understand his own innermost being that he will fall on his face, worship God and recognize that God is in fact in our midst."[49]

I found this argument a little strange. I had never felt like falling on my face and declaring that God was in our midst. This did not bother me, but I still found it strange that they believed that their crucified Jesus was both in their midst and that he would come again. To my way of understanding, these were two very obvious contradictions. On the other hand I was not disturbed by the singing in tongues and the emotional outbreaks from Chloe. On the contrary, the human, sometimes almost primitive spontaneity of the Christian worship, and their direct way of dealing with each other, impressed me.

Peace with a Difference
I do not know why, but all at once there was complete silence in the villa. Almost everyone sat with his or her eyes closed. They prayed in silence. Erastus stood at the table

with the scroll in his hands, flanked by the two torch-bearers. I could not say whether this silence lasted for moments or for half an hour. Suddenly I felt something rising in me. At first I thought that I was going to vomit. But it was something else. I feared that I was going to weep in the middle of this awful silence. And I did not know why. In desperation I grasped a corner of my tunic and put it in my mouth. I do not really know what happened to me. It is of course true that I do not have a proper identity. I do not know where I belong. The old Greek religion has been so changed by the occupation of the Romans that it is almost unrecognizable. It does not speak to me. The Oriental mystery religions are too Saturnalian for my taste and the synagogues of the Jews too strict. I cannot feel one with the uneducated slaves, and the more educated people in Corinth (even if they would accept me) are too superficial. If I could have it my way I would like to be a free-floating religionless skeptic. Then my status as a secretary-slave would not bother me. Can one live like that? As an agnostic—especially if one is committed to a bank?

The Christians sang again their hymn "And now abideth...." "And now abideth faith," some sang, while others continued, "And now abideth hope." A third group added, "And now abideth love." Then all three groups joined together to sing, "But the greatest of these is love."[50]

Too good to be true, I thought.

Erastus continued his reading, but it no longer interested me. He read, "Of the prophets, two or three may speak, while the rest exercise their judgment upon what is said."[51] Erastus stopped. "The others shall exercise their judgment," Tertius repeated. "That means, for instance, when Chloe is prophesying that we, the others, who have also received the Holy Spirit, evaluate her prophecy. It means when Paul writes a letter to us that we exercise our judgment on whether or not we can recognize God's will in his writings. The others are those who confirm the inspiration of a prophet, a teacher, a writer—or reject it."

Erastus continued from Paul's letter: "If someone else, sitting in his place, receives a revelation, let the first speaker stop."[52] "Amen, amen," the slaves shouted. Erastus went on, "You can all prophesy, one at a time, so that the whole congregation may receive instruction and encouragement. Prophetic outbreaks are subject to the control of the prophet, for the God who inspires them is not a God of disorder but of peace."[53]

A strange ending, I thought. Paul did not write, "God is not a God of disorder but of order." He did not go so far as to identify himself with the apostles of "law and order," with the port authorities and against the rioting slaves. He did not speak of "order" but of "peace." On our way home I asked Tertius how he understood that final sentence.

"Order," Tertius said, "can only be understood hierarchically and statically, as a power which rules over others. That is not what Paul means. For Paul 'peace' means to name and suffer conflicts—sometimes even to live a long time with them—without destroying the community in the body of the Lord. Peace means that we recognize Chloe to be an organ in this body, even if she makes us suffer sometimes. And obviously we make her suffer too."

"And what do you think about that alleged insertion concerning the place of women in the meeting of the Christians?" I asked him this in regard to Chloe.

He replied, "I wrote a letter for Paul once about three years ago. It was addressed to the Christians in Rome. I wrote it without charging any fee,[54] for Paul's and Christ's sake. During and after dictation he got me to alter the wording quite a lot. Sometimes he told me to cross out whole passages and reword them. So it is not impossible that he also wrote this passage. But I must say that the style

33

does not sound at all like his, and the statements certainly are in contradiction to other things he had written. But then Paul is not a very logical writer. On the whole I would agree with Chloe. It seems unlikely to me that Paul wrote this passage himself. Somebody, possibly a well-meaning secretary, has put it in. Perhaps the letter has been read already to another house church in Corinth, and maybe they have added this section. We are going to write to Paul and ask him about it."

Shall I Become a Christian?

We said good-bye and I returned alone through the night streets of Corinth. I live in a small room in a villa belonging to one of the directors of the bank where I am employed. There I keep the few things which belong to me—a second tunic, sandals, parchment, a bed and a lamp. Every day I go to the office in the bank. I am responsible for checking transactions and general bookkeeping, and I have to make sure that letters of credit and coins are always correctly filed and put away, especially in the evening when the bank is closed. In uncertain times, as had been the case this week, I have to work overtime. Once or twice a year on the great public holidays we close the bank for a whole day. The Corinthians drink so much that it is advisable to close and see that the bank is securely locked up.

I am a slave and my master is a director of the Corinthian Bank of Trade and Commerce. He treats me well. I have enough to eat and a small room. When I need anything I can go to him. Only I do not know where I belong. I do not belong to the free businessmen, the officers, the scientists, and the bankers, nor do I belong to the slaves and dock workers who—so they say—think not merely with the head but with the whole body. Perhaps, if I am lucky, I will be given my freedom one day. It happens sometimes, but it depends on the good will of one's master.

And so I ask myself whether or not the citizens'

meeting of the Christians is the right place for me.

I cannot be a whole human being all on my own. I need Chloe's people and also Erastus and Gaius and my friend Tertius. But being a Christian has great disadvantages. Christians run the risk of being regarded as non-conformist or even hostile to the state. That is because so many of the Christians are slaves. Numerically slaves are in the majority. But they do not have as much influence as the minority of free and affluent Christians. Membership in the body of the Christians means a tremendous increase in prestige for the slaves. But as I have already said, to be a Christian has disadvantages. One could easily be identified with Chloe's people, and if one is arrested and convicted of conspiracy it does not really matter whether one is guilty or not. A just conviction or a miscarriage of justice produces the same result. One is dead.

What shall I do?

Is there any good reason for becoming a Christian?

Do I need any reason for becoming a Christian?

MEMOIRS OF AN OLD MAN

MY NAME IS SERAIAH. I was born in the same year as the battle that was waged at Carchemish between the Babylonian Crown Prince Nebuchadnezzar and the Egyptian Pharaoh Neco.[1] The tiny state of Judah had joined a western economic and military alliance under Egyptian leadership. Judah put their faith in Pharaoh whose mobile commando units offered protection from the eastern powers. Things didn't turn out as they had hoped. The prediction of the prophet Jeremiah was to be fulfilled. He had prophesied: The sword will eat up the crack troops of the western military alliance. It will be drunk with their blood. The Lord will hold an orgy of slaughter. Thus spoke Jeremiah and thus it came to pass.[2] Jerusalem was stripped of its western military shield. She became a satellite state of Babylon.[3] When Judah rebelled eight years later, Nebuchadnezzar moved against the city, destroyed it and sent the ruling families, the civil servants, the educated elite and the priests into exile in Babylon.

As an eight-year-old lad I went to live in the neighborhood of Nippur.[4] When I turned sixteen my father put me into an apprenticeship in the famous and influential merchant bank, Murashu & Sons Ltd.,[5] which had its head office in Nippur. There I learned cuneiform script, cuneiform bookkeeping and the neo-Babylonian language. I found the script rather difficult because the

Babylonians do not use letters the way we Jews do, but use a syllabic script. However, the language is easy and is related to ours.

After I had served my apprenticeship I was made a manager in the foreign exchange section of Murashu & Sons Ltd. I received a steady salary. As Jewish prisoners our freedom of movement was somewhat limited, in that we had to have a pass to visit another city, but by and large we were treated fairly. We were allowed to practice our religion, we lived in our own houses and could cultivate gardens,[6] and we organized ourselves into a Jewish Union.[7]

As I was only eight years old at the time, I myself have only faint recollections of the deportation, of Jerusalem before the exile, and of the temple as it was.

Only one thing sticks indelibly in my mind about that long march from Jerusalem to Nippur, and that is the priests who carried great mountains of documents and scrolls on their backs. Once I walked for a long time behind a priest's son. His name was Ezekiel. It was obvious that he was more accustomed to writing than carrying loads, and he often had to put down the scrolls and take a rest. Once, when he was sitting down, I asked him why he was putting himself to so much trouble for these documents which were already somewhat scorched by fire. He gave me a long look. Then he said: "Look, young fellow, I saved these fragments of holy writings from the burning temple because the Word must not be lost; it must be preserved. We can do without food and clothing; in dire circumstances we can even manage without the temple. But without the Word we are lost."

There is not much to tell about my youth in Babylon. I stayed with Murashu & Sons Ltd. It wasn't a bad job. From time to time a beautiful young girl came into our foreign exchange office. She was called Esther and was the daughter of one of the directors of the bank. I grew to like her very much and had reason to believe that the feeling was mutual. I was then twenty-three years old and would have liked to marry Esther, but she was a Babylonian. My father had reservations about marriage with a "heathen," as he put it. But the Babylonians, or, as my father used to say, "the heathen," were, in my eyes at least, an educated and civilized people. Not only was Babylon the leading economic and military power, but it also led the world in science and the arts. The internationalism of the Babylonians was illuminating. Their moral law was not barbarian, in spite of what my father liked to say.

By the Waters of Babylon

To take my mind off Esther and all things Babylonian, my father used to take me with him regularly to the Jewish wakes. One of these wakes made a particularly deep impression on me. I had put away the cuneiform tablets with the exchange rates for the week and taken my leave of Esther. My father was waiting for me outside the bank and we went together to the river Chebar.[8] This river Chebar (in Accadian, Nar Kabari) was an important meeting place for the Jews. Nearby, in Tel Abubi, that is, the Hill of the Flood, lived Ezekiel. This Ezekiel knew more about the history of our people than anyone else, except perhaps one of his colleagues whom we called "the priest" and whose real name I never could remember.

People said that Ezekiel had even eaten a book[9]—a real bookworm. He was at the same time attractive and repulsive. According to my father, he once built a model of the city of Jerusalem out of tiles before the eyes of the baffled citizens. Then he collected together small scale siege machines. He shattered the wall, placing siege towers and battering rams against it. And then he set up a regular "sit-in." He built his model in the High Street in Jerusalem and lay on the ground next to it for one hundred and ninety days, that is, longer than half a year. The people of

41

Jerusalem shook their heads and said he had gone mad. He lay there on the ground for half a year, they said, contemplating his siege model, doing absolutely no work, behaving more childishly than a child, and on top of that he claimed that this was part of his commission as a prophet of Yahweh. But he did not stop there. He dramatically illustrated the day-to-day worsening of the situation in the besieged city by every day baking a smaller loaf, for which he carefully measured out just enough flour. To bring home to them the shortage of wood, he baked it on cow dung. At that time everybody laughed at the madman. But this his prophecy came true in every detail.[10]

As we came to the river Chebar, we could hear the lamentations of the Jews in the distance. In a deep monotone, always singing in the same key, the men began:[11]

"By the waters of Babylon...."

Then they drew a breath and started again half a tone higher:

"By the waters of Babylon...."

Countless times they sang one after another:

"By the waters of Babylon...."

And then it broke like a howling storm:

"By the waters of Babylon we sat and wept...."

After a long pause they added softly:

"We leave our harps hanging
Hanging on the willow trees there
For there they required of us a song,
They who had taken us captive
And in our anguish required of us mirth."

In fact some Babylonians who were enjoying the cool evening wind sometimes called out to the Jews: "Hey, sing us one of the latest songs of Zion." But the Jews did not want to sing to entertain the Babylonians, and certainly not to sing a song of Zion.

We approached a group of Jews in the twilight. My colleagues from the bank were standing a little apart. Most of them had been born in exile and could only speak broken Hebrew. They had once told me that the Jewish lamentation psalms meant nothing to them. It was obvious that they would rather have gone to a festival in a Babylonian temple, and not only because of the Babylonian girls. Basically it suited them in Babylon and they did not feel homesick for the backwoods of Judah. In their eyes Babylon was a much more exciting place. They often gossiped during the psalms and got drunk, breaking open the wineskins they had brought with them, and squirting wine into each other's mouths.

Tabaoth and the Faith of the Fathers

Prominent among those singing laments was Tabaoth, an old man whose forefathers had been temple servants. He had thin white hair and an equally thin white beard. In Babylon he was the leader of the "Save Our Religious Heritage Movement," called "Sourem" for short. As we came up, he was repeating what he had often said before: "Unshaken we hold fast to the faith of our fathers, to the faith of ancient Israel, namely: to the creation of the world as a garden of paradise in the midst of the desert; the exodus from Egypt and the miraculous journey through the wilderness; Moses the lawgiver inspired by God; David

43

and his eternal throne; the temple in Jerusalem as the center of the world."

The young Murashu employees grinned as he came out with this confession of faith. My colleague Abu-Banini (that is a Babylonian name and means "Abu has begotten me") said: "According to this creed we were led out of Egypt six hundred years ago. Can you explain to me then why, six hundred years after our liberation from the Egyptians, we should expect these very same Egyptians to rescue us from the Babylonians? Why do you and your friends keep looking out of the corner of your eye at the west and hoping that the western commando units will make a lightning raid to rescue you from the Babylonians? You could wait for a long time because Egypt is so corrupt that she cannot lead a war against the strong eastern powers. Egypt is a reed. It stabs the hands of those who lean on it."[12]

The old man, Tabaoth, listened with a bowed head and said nothing.

Now, however, a second Murashu employee tackled him. He was called Eannadu.

"You speak of Moses, the divinely inspired lawgiver. With all due respect, we do not dispute the ethical value of the Ten Commandments, but the Ten Commandments of the ancient Babylonian King Hammurabi are older than the Mosaic tables of the law and are certainly not inferior. And how you can go on and on about David's eternal throne and the temple in Jerusalem as the center of the world—I don't know."

"Young man, hold your tongue," shouted my father, getting all worked up. "Do not blaspheme against the Holy City, against the temple, against the Anointed One of God, the king of David's stock."

"Ho, ho," laughed Eannadu. "David was no more than a cunning rascal and a shrewd operator who used the breathing space given him by the great powers for his career of robbery and his dynastic marriages. Moreover, why make such a song and dance whenever we flirt with Babylonian girls? David himself married many such women whom you call 'heathen.' Why should something be sacred for him which is taboo for us?"

"And anyway," Abu-Banini now took up the thread, "the royal house of David has been crushed. Isn't the last king of David's line, Joachim, Nebuchadnezzar's prisoner?[13] And doesn't the temple lie in ruins? And doesn't Yahweh share his residence with bats and jackals— doesn't he?"

The old man said only: "The faith of our fathers meets all needs." And then he was silent for a long time.

The Space Engineer
In the meantime it had grown dark. Four great torches were lit and someone called out: "Priest, why don't you say something?"

The priest answered: "If you are prepared to listen, I am willing to speak."

"Speak," everyone cried.

"The faith of our fathers did meet all needs," the priest asserted now, and looked at Tabaoth, who nodded his head. "It did meet their needs then, but today it no longer does so. Let us take the first point in our creed, the creation of the world by Yahweh as a garden of paradise in the desert. Every child in Babylon today knows that this wasn't the way things happened at the beginning. Our fathers were nomads. They could only understand the world as an oasis in the desert. Today we know that the world is a hemisphere, enclosed by transparent hemispherical glass, surrounded above and below by the waters of primeval chaos. The Babylonians call it 'Thiamat.' We say 'Themot.' "

"But you know full well," my father interposed now, "that the Babylonians believe 'Thiamat' is a goddess who threatens man's existence with her flood-waters. We need only a tiny porthole in the vaults of heaven or a door in the world's floor to be open a crack and the goddess of chaos would drown us in the water. At least that is how the Babylonians explain the flood. And this belief in the all-powerful goddess who can only be restrained by perpetual sacrifices is paganism which we must strictly forswear."

"But what if it is true?" Abu-Banini interjected. "What if it is true?"

"What is true?" the priest began again.[14] "What is true is that the world is encased in water. How the Babylonians, with their obsession for the latest scientific theories, can believe that this water is a goddess is beyond my comprehension. They have never proved it. Abu-Banini, come here!"

Abu-Banini went up to the priest, who told him: "Hold your hand in the Chebar canal!" Abu-Banini held his hand in the canal. "What do you feel?" the priest asked.

"I feel water," the young man answered.

"Aha, you feel water. You do not feel a goddess," the priest commented. The young man began to laugh uncomfortably. "Look here," continued the priest. "The Babylonians are not critical enough as scientists. The waters of chaos, whose blue color we can see through the glass globe, if we look toward heaven, are water. Only there is much more of it than there is in the Chebar canal. And these waters are held in their place by Yahweh. And they will stay there forever.

"Exactly the same thing holds good for the heavenly bodies," the priest went on.[15] " 'Shamash' and 'Sin,' sun and moon, are not, as the Babylonians infer, independent heavenly powers but lamps created by Yahweh. A large lamp for daytime so that it will be fully light, and a small bedside light for the night. Yahweh has designed an apparatus to program these lamps so that they do not give light at the wrong time or get switched off. And you can see for yourselves how well the system works. It has been so from the beginning and will last forever. Yahweh ordered it so. And he has given us understanding so that we can understand it and him, Yahweh, and thus give him thanks and honor."

"But what is Yahweh doing the whole day then, since the world is running like clockwork?" one of Tabaoth's disciples asked.

"I do not know," the priest answered. "Presumably he is having a rest. He is observing the sabbath."

"What a terrible picture of God you are painting for us," Tabaoth complained. "Is that the God who led his people through the wilderness? Is this our God Yahweh, the God of Abraham, Isaac and Jacob? A clever watchmaker, nothing more? If I have got your explanation right—and I can understand very little of it, also I am too old—how can one pray anymore to this computer-God? He is clever, of course, but has he a heart? I can only protest against this transformation of Yahweh into a space engineer. I stick to my conviction: the faith of the fathers still meets all our needs."

His young colleague added: "Our 'Save Our Religious Heritage Movement' Sourem must boycott the theology of the priest. He is more dangerous than the people in Murashu & Sons Ltd., with their shopkeepers' minds who have become Babylonianized. The priest and his followers are more dangerous than the Babylonians themselves, since they are perverting the faith. At least we, at our 'Festival of Scripture Truth' which will take place soon, shall see to it that the writings of the priest are treated the same way as the wretched defeatist tract which Jeremiah sent to us in Babylon over ten years ago,[16] when he had the audacity to ask for our loyalty to the Babylonians. They shall be accursed!"

"Accursed!" the people from the Sourem-movement

repeated. "Let all those people be accursed who under-mine our simple faith with sophisticated philosophizing. Let all those be accursed who complicate the simple truth with Babylonian hair-splitting!"

"You may ignore the truth," the priest answered in a steely voice. "But you cannot defeat the truth. It is not my fault that the truth is not always simple."

I was unhappy about the tone of the debate. Some-thing did not quite fit. It was obvious that old Tabaoth was unable to follow the priest's train of thought. He argued as best he could but he lacked the necessary knowledge of Accadian language and culture. It seemed to me that this conflict had not only religious but also social and cultural connotations. The people from the "Save Our Religious Heritage Movement" saw themselves as guardians of the truth and were put off by the rational style of the priest's theology, even if he himself did not consider his theology to be as rationalistic as his audience did. It is possible that the priest regarded old Tabaoth as somewhat limited in his understanding. Certainly that was the case with the Murashu lot. But was it Tabaoth's fault that he could not find any point of contact with the Babylonian philosophy?

Ezekiel and a New Heart
I remembered that at the risk of his own life Ezekiel had saved the old scrolls from the temple and carried them to Babylon. He would certainly not have done that if they had been worth nothing. I asked Ezekiel, who was sitting there silently, why he said nothing. Ezekiel responded: "If you are prepared to listen, I am willing to speak."

The pro-Babylonian party of young men shouted: "Speak, Ezekiel. You are a good speaker—as good as, if not better than, the Babylonian orators."[17] Tabaoth signed and Ezekiel got up. He shook his head. He had a narrow, pale face which appeared even whiter than usual in the light of the torches. He folded his hands and one could see that his fingers were constantly shaking.

"It is true," he now began, "that the faith of our fathers met all their needs. But it does not do so anymore for us. Do you realize that the Babylonians do not understand us?"

"It is not necessary for them to understand us," my father protested. "The heathen do not understand the faith."

Ezekiel looked at my father and added softly, "Our own young people also laugh at us." I could feel myself blushing to the roots of my hair. Luckily it was dark and my father could not see. "They laugh mistakenly," Ezekiel continued, and his eyes swept over Abu-Banini and Eannadu, who remained silent.

"That will only change," he continued, "if we ourselves change along with our faith and our theology. Something completely new must emerge: a new spirit, a new heart! With regard to the old theology, which is bound up with the city of Jerusalem, the land of Israel, the land of Yahweh, we can only say from our exile here: Our bones are dried up. Our hope is gone. We are as good as dead."[18]

The young people laughed again, but the congregation broke into another song of lamentation which they already knew well: "Our bones are dried up...." They sang it to the same tune as "By the waters of Babylon." Then they added another verse to it:

> "Our fathers have eaten sour grapes
> And our teeth are set on edge.
> We are being punished for the sins of our
>   fathers
> To the third and fourth generation."[19]

"What nonsense!" mocked Abu-Banini as Ezekiel continued:

"We must live in an impure land
and eat impure bread
since there is no pure bread here."[20]

Abu-Banini whispered to me: "Babylonian bread is not as bad as all that."

Ezekiel, however, went on: "What use is it to assert that all we need is faith in the temple? It is in ruins. The only hope for us is that a new temple will be built. A new, different temple will be given to us. And that will happen not because some conservatives hold that the faith of the fathers meets all our needs at all times and hold fast to the old traditions, but because Yahweh has decided it so. He has decided not to be disgraced by his people. He will see to it that he is known and revered by those who did not know him before, or did not know him properly."[21] Tabaoth sighed and shook his head and repeated: "The faith of the fathers meets all our needs. You, Ezekiel, with your modern theology, are more dangerous than the young people. They speak without understanding. But you teach a new doctrine and you know what you are doing." Then all alone, in a quavering thin voice, he sang:

"Our bones are dried up,
Our hope is gone.
We are as good as dead,
As good as dead."[22]

Resurrection
Nobody said a word. Ezekiel had closed his eyes. Softly, but clearly and audibly, he began again:[23]

"The hand of Yahweh is upon me
And he carries me away by the spirit of Yahweh
And sets me down in the middle of a valley,
A valley full of dry bones

50

Lying round about, in great numbers
Covering the earth.
And behold they are very dry.
And he says to me:
'Son of man, can these bones live again?'
And I answer:
'You know, O Lord Yahweh.'
But he says to me:
'Prophesy over these dry bones and say to
    them:
O dry bones, hear the word of Yahweh.
Thus Yahweh speaks to these bones:
See, I am going to breathe the spirit of life
    into you
And put flesh on you and draw skin over
    you,
And give life to you, so that you can become
    alive.
And you shall know that I am Yahweh.' "

Ezekiel took a deep breath. Some were secretly wiping
their eyes. He continued:

"And now there is a noise,
behold, a sound of clattering.
And the bones are joined together, one to
    another
and behold, there are sinews
and the flesh grows on them
and skin is drawn under and over them
but there is no breath of life in them.
Now the Lord speaks to me:
'Prophesy, son of man, say about the spirit of
    life:
Thus says Yahweh:
Come from the four winds, O spirit of life,

breathe on these dead souls here
and let them live again.'
And so I prophesy.
And the spirit of life falls upon them
and they come to life and stand on their feet,
a great, great army."

Old Tabaoth repeated slowly: "A great, great army."

One of my colleagues jumped in and asked: "Ezekiel, you speak in riddles.[24] What does this mean, then?"

I was taken aback when I heard my father answering. He said: "The bones are the house of Israel. The Lord is opening our grave and our prison and is bringing us back to Jerusalem."[25]

Isaiah the Younger and the Messiah

Fifty years have now passed since that thought-provoking vision at the river Chebar. I am now an old man. Ezekiel and the priest are dead. However, their words have been written down. I myself helped to preserve and interpret them.

I have now been back in Jerusalem for many years. The Persian Shah Cyrus conquered Babylon and ordered us to return to Jerusalem.

On the rise to power of the Persian kings, one of our younger prophets in exile, Isaiah the Younger, alerted us to the worldwide significance of this young warrior and statesman, Cyrus. With the turnabout in the struggle for political power which brought Cyrus onto the stage of world history, Isaiah the Younger told us: "This is the beginning of the end." In Yahweh's name he called out in Babylon: "I bring my victory near, my salvation will not tarry. Yahweh bares his arm before the eyes of the people."[26]

Of Cyrus, Isaiah the Younger said: "From the north I have aroused him, and he came from the rising of the sun, he who calls on my name, and he smashed princes like clay figures, like a potter crushing clay." Yahweh has given Cyrus a free hand in world history. He will shatter iron bars and hidden treasures will fall into his hands.[27] He, whom Yahweh loves, that is Cyrus, lays siege to Babylon and lets the prisoners go home 'without ransom money and without bribes.'[28] Therefore Isaiah the Younger also called him the Messiah, or the Christ,[29] a claim which caused many eyebrows to be raised to heaven, since how could a Persian king take up the messianic inheritance of David?

His refrain "Comfort ye, comfort ye my people"[30] impressed us all. When he spoke about our return, which was to be on a way cleared of obstacles, we rejoiced.[31] He promised us that we would no longer know hunger or thirst, and that the darkness would become light.[32] The mountains would break into shouts of praise and the trees would clap their hands[33] when the redeemed of Yahweh return home. The heathen will acknowledge the powerlessness of their gods. They will be ashamed of themselves.[34] They will come to Yahweh. "Kings will see it, and stand up, and princes will prostrate themselves."[35]

Not one of us has forgotten the song that he taught us and which has become our family prayer:

> "For a small moment have I forsaken thee
> But with great mercies will I gather thee.
> For the mountains shall depart and the
>   hills be removed
> But my kindness shall not depart from thee,
> Neither shall the covenant of my peace be
>   removed."[36]

It is true that Yahweh remained silent while our enemies triumphed over us. But how he had to restrain himself and hid his anguish![37] No one should think that Yahweh had cast off his people in a fury. "Where is your decree of divorce?" Isaiah the Younger asked us, and we had to answer: "There is none."[38] Yahweh has forgiven us, his people.

I must confess that I did not entirely believe the prophet. It seemed to me too wonderful. But when Cyrus really did overpower the kingdom of Croesus like a whirlwind and when the military might of the Babylonians collapsed before his advance,[39] then we said to one another: "He is right. Yahweh has not forgotten us."

Then there came that memorable moment when the Persian king, whom Isaiah called the Christ, promulgated his edict, in which he ordered the temple to be rebuilt in Jerusalem with the aid of the Persian government. The temple furnishings confiscated and desecrated by Nebuchadnezzar were brought out of the treasury in Babylon and taken back to Jerusalem.[40] All this was too wonderful for us. Cyrus even sent an official, named Sheshbazzar,[41] who soon laid the foundations of the new temple. We witnessed a marvelous economic, political and religious miracle.

I myself went back to Jerusalem with both my sons and with my Babylonian wife, Esther, who had espoused the Jewish faith for my sake. Together with my sons, I took over a small branch office of Murashu & Sons Ltd. in Jerusalem. As Accadian became more and more unfashionable, Aramaic developed as the new business language. Persian was the language of our new masters but I could not manage to learn it at my age. My sons, however, were already well versed in it.

Haggai and the Building of the Temple
And yet here in Jerusalem it is not all sweetness and light. Last week I was inspecting the temple area. It is true, the foundations have been laid. But grass is growing over them, for the building work stopped four years ago. Where then are the great hopes of Ezekiel and Isaiah the Younger?

In the temple area was a young man, also one of those

who had returned from Babylon. He is called Haggai. He reproached me, shouting: "You mean to say that the time has not yet come to rebuild the house of the Lord? Has the time come to live in paneled houses while this house lies in ruins?"[42]

Before all the people he criticized me as if it were my duty to build the temple, as if the prophets had not promised that he, Yahweh, or at least the Persian governor would initiate it. "No wonder," Haggai continued, "that everything slips between your fingers in that heathen bank of yours so that your sons shake their heads over you. You looked for much, and lo, it came to little. Why is that? I ask you. I will tell you: Because my house lies in ruins, says Yahweh, while each of you delights in his own house."[43]

I shook my head. I could make nothing of it. But it was a bad day for me because one of Haggai's disciples joined the debate—well, to be exact, it was not a debate but rather a haranguing of an old man by a young religious fanatic. This young man asked me: "Do your sons know any Hebrew at all? Do they know the law? Yes, they have studied Persian and Accadian and even the latest modern folly, Greek language and philosophy. But have they studied the law of Yahweh? That is the result of a man making a fool of himself and marrying a foreign wife, as you have done. Were decent Jewish women not good enough for you that you let yourself be seduced by an exotic woman?"

"Young man," I answered him calmly, "one does not speak to an old man like that in Israel. That is also stated in the law."

"But what if the old man has forgotten the law?" he answered, stretching out his hand and trying to pull my beard. However, Haggai restrained him.[44]

I went home sadly. "The new Jerusalem, the new temple," I thought, "but their hearts are still the old hearts and their quarrels are still the same old quarrels; and all I have done in marrying Esther the Babylonian is to do what the prophet Jeremiah told us to do."[45]

The Peace To Come

Returning home, I found both my sons involved in a lively discussion with a client. Because the discussion looked as though it had been going on for a long time, I invited all three to drink a "sundowner" in my house. It turned out that the stranger was a scholar from Isaiah's school. They make copies of and commentaries on the writings of Isaiah the Elder and Isaiah the Younger. I was naturally interested in how someone you might call a specialist on Isaiah's prophecies could reconcile these prophecies with the simple fact that we had returned to Jerusalem but the "light" had not shone forth in the way the prophet and his disciples had promised.

We seated ourselves at the stone table outside our house. Esther set a flagon of wine in the middle and sat down a little to one side. Our guest sat next to me, and opposite us sat my sons. The younger of them opened the discussion and said pointedly: "That we came back to Jerusalem is not exactly a miracle. It was in the interest of the Persian Minister of Religious Affairs. The God Yahweh may well exist, but he does not take any interest in us since he hardly ever intervenes in our history. Perhaps he has forgotten us."

"Not true," retorted the guest. "The hand of Yahweh is not too short to help us, and his ear is not so deaf that he cannot hear, but our sins separate us from our God. Man trusts in vanity." Here he looked over to our little bank office. "You get pregnant with disaster."[46]

"That's laying it on a bit," my younger son jumped in, and his brother commented: "Come on, now. Admittedly our young satellite state, created by the good pleasure of Persia, is very new. The conflict with the Samaritans, who stayed behind and wanted to take part in the rebuilding of the temple, could erupt into a civil war. But what else could we do? These are normal difficulties of a young state."

"Indeed," I said, lapsing into the kind of depression that afflicts one at my time of life, "we do not know the way of peace, neither for our fellow believers who returned from Babylon nor for those who stayed behind. We roar like bears, we sigh like doves. We wait for justice and it does not come. We grope around like blind people along a wall. We stumble in the bright midday sun as if it were already dusk. We sit in darkness like the dead."[47]

My sons winked at each other as if they wanted to say: He's off again. Then our guest said, "A vivid picture." My wife joined in. She set a fresh cup of wine in front of each of us and then asked: "Can my lords not put it more concretely? What is meant by 'the way of peace' which you do not know?"

My guest stared at me reproachfully. Apparently he was not accustomed to having women share in a discussion with men, and particularly not a foreign woman. But Esther's question was indeed the most pertinent one in the world.

"Now the way of peace would be a solution to our housing problem," I replied. "It is well known how many men here in Jerusalem must live in ruined cellars and miserable holes. Above all, it is those who stayed behind who suffer, while we, the returned exiles, because of our contacts with our overlords, can erect proper houses quickly. Somehow that doesn't seem right." No one said anything. "Yes, my friend," I asked the guest, "what do you say to that?"

My guest had not been listening. He sat there with closed eyes. I was reminded of Ezekiel at the Chebar riverside. Finally he said softly:

"The sons of strangers will build up your walls,

And their kings shall minister unto you.
Your gates will stand open at all times.
Day and night they will not be closed
So that the wealth of the nations may be brought
  in to you.
Your sun will set no more
Nor your moon wane.
Your people will all be righteous
And possess the land forever.
I, Yahweh, have spoken.
I will hasten it in due time."[48]

"Wishful thinking!" my sons mocked, lifting their cups and draining them. Nobody had any wish to continue the conversation, so my guest took his leave. My sons went peacefully to sleep. My wife lit a small oil lamp for me and I took parchment and a reed and wrote out this my story. I wrote it for myself and also for my sons. About dawn I read my memoirs out loud to my wife who, without saying a word, had stayed awake with me.

She said: "The conclusion is missing. What have you learned in your life?"

I had to think about that for a long time. I had to ask myself whether those were right who had promised us that we could experience God in worship, in the temple, in the law and finally in the history of Yahweh with his people, in our return to Jerusalem. Are they right? Or is Yahweh only to be experienced *beyond* all our experiences? What a fascinating question!

I asked Esther if our life is already the resurrection of the dry bones which Ezekiel promised us: "Is this the new Israel, the new temple of which Ezekiel spoke? The miniature temple which is being built—if it is ever finished—makes a poor show, compared with the former temple of Solomon, or with the Babylonian and Persian temples. Jealousy and quarrels erupt between rich and poor, and the theological war between the citizens of

Jerusalem and the Samaritans has grown more bitter. Is that the new age of which the prophet spoke, or must we still wait for it?"

Esther's Postscript

My husband did not have to wait much longer. One week after he had finished his memoirs, he died. He went during the night. When I tried to wake him up in the morning, he did not reply. He lay there, stiff, immovable, almost like the corpses in Ezekiel's vision; there was no life in him anymore.

The usual Jewish mourners came to the funeral, most of them his relations. They wailed and lamented. In the speeches at the wake, the oldest among them reminded us of his work as copyist and interpreter of Ezekiel, his role as a mediator in Babylon, and his reliable work in the bank of Murashu & Sons Ltd., which was important for the re-construction of Jerusalem. It seemed to me that now, even more than during his life, he was becoming the public property of the Jewish religious leaders.

Of my sons, who were still his sons too, no one said anything, and certainly nothing was said about me, because I was just tolerated as an unclean, heathen woman in the midst of the chosen people.

However, I am going to complete the memoirs of my husband for his sons, since they are my sons too, and it seems important to me that they should also receive their mother's inheritance when I am no longer here. My husband wrote his memoirs in Hebrew, using the Hebrew script. I can read that well, and my sons can read it more or less. However, I myself write Accadian in cuneiform script because it is and will remain my mother tongue. I bear the name of a Babylonian goddess. She is called Ishtar in Accadian, Esther in Hebrew. The fact that I have the name of a Babylonian goddess gave rise to arguments and ugly scenes in Babylon and even more so here in Jerusalem.

One such row I remember particularly well. We had been in Jerusalem only a year or two. Two couriers came from Egypt. They brought important documents from the Egyptian subsidiary of Murashu & Sons Ltd. in Elephantine. After the business was completed they came to our house. They had to spend the night with us because it was too late to continue their journey to the head office of the bank in Nippur. While I prepared supper, I heard the first, who was called Ben-Baruch, talking about Egypt. For the first time in my life I learned that there was a Jewish settlement in Egypt and that—like Ezekiel in Babylon—Jeremiah stayed with the exiles and admonished them with his prophecies. Ben-Baruch was the son of Jeremiah's private secretary and was therefore very well informed about public and domestic affairs in Egypt.

He said to my husband: "Can you imagine, Seraiah, that in Egypt many of our womenfolk pray to the Queen of Heaven. Sacred totem posts were erected here in Israel long ago in her honor,[49] and the prophets campaigned against this with all their might. They called it the Canaanite abomination and the Babylonian disgrace. Baruch, my father, has written about this. The men used to support their wives in this abominable cult. The women said to Jeremiah: We are not going to listen to what you, Jeremiah, tell us in the name of the Lord. We are going to keep our vows in that we will make sacrifices and pour out drink-offerings to the Queen of Heaven, as we and our fathers, our kings and lords in the cities of Judah and the streets of Jerusalem, used to do. Then we had enough bread and were prosperous and misfortune did not touch us. Since we have stopped offering sacrifices and drink-offerings, we have suffered all sorts of things and we know hunger and the sword. Whenever we bake cakes (cakes which are in the shape of the goddess), do you really think we do this without the consent of our menfolk?"[50]

I was at the oven in the middle of baking cakes, but I

heard every word that Ben-Baruch pronounced. My husband asked him: "And what did Jeremiah say in reply?"

"You can imagine his anger when he put them right," Ben-Baruch replied. " 'It is exactly the opposite,' Jeremiah told the Jews. 'Everything went wrong for you because you have worshiped a goddess besides Yahweh. If it must be so, that you run after this wanton goddess, why not become completely heathen and give up worshiping Yahweh altogether? To worship Yahweh and the Queen of Heaven at the same time—that is out of the question.' "

My husband did not reply. "Esther," he called, "is the meal ready?"

I carried in the cakes made with fine white flour, together with vegetables and mutton. My husband spoke the blessing, and I sat down a little apart from my husband and the two guests according to the Jewish custom and ate with my sons, who were not yet grown men.

Unexpectedly, the younger of the two guests, whose name I can't remember anymore, said: "Esther—isn't that a Babylonian name?"

"Of course," my husband answered. "My wife is a Babylonian, but for my sake she adopted the Jewish faith."

"Esther!" the younger one went on, and took care not to look in my direction. "Esther! Esther is a beautiful Babylonian goddess of spring of whom it is said that every spring she goes down into the underworld, passes through seven doors, and at each door gives up a piece of her clothing until she stands in dazzling nakedness before the goddess of the underworld. I have seen pictures of this Babylonian goddess, and really—she is a beautiful woman. Then, the story goes, after being put through many tests and trials, she bathes in the source of life and comes back to earth where she sets the new spring going. In the statues which I have seen, she holds a little boy in her arm who suckles her breasts. A fascinating picture of the ever returning resurrection!"[51]

"Don't you know," Ben-Baruch now asked him, "what awful scenes take place in the Babylonian temples as part of this cult of the goddess? Don't you know that in her temples so-called sacred priestesses couple with the priests in a so-called holy marriage in order to celebrate the return of the goddess Ishtar?"[52]

The young man apparently knew nothing of this, but he was not shocked. Dryly he retorted, to Ben-Baruch's astonishment: "I have seen worse things, such as when the Jews tear each other's hair for the sake of some interpretation of the law, when they compete for a position in the Egyptian provincial government or when they curse their own prophets and mock them."

"Enough!" Ben-Baruch said, raising his voice. "A woman as God is unthinkable for a Jew! Yahweh is the father of his people and not the mother!"

"Why not?" I ventured to say, but the guests did not take my question up. Only my husband said: "But there is also a tradition in Israel in which it is said that Yahweh loves his people as a mother loves her child.[53] So that idea is not completely excluded. And the fact that we can understand Yahweh only as being a man and not as a man and a woman is also the reason for the harshness and uncompromising attitude of our religion."

"But perhaps not," Ben-Baruch retorted, "since our faith has stood firm and is not like the women's cults around us, adapting to every new wind, every new fashion."

Ben-Baruch was nevertheless tactful enough to refrain from criticizing my husband. After all, he was our guest. But it was obvious that to him a Jew who married a Babylonian was beyond the pale—and, more than that, he had married one with the name of a pagan goddess.

I noticed particularly that Ben-Baruch had hurt my husband with his condemnation of everything Babylonian, or, as he said, everything pagan. When we were alone, I said to him: "Seraiah, among the Jews too, we need men who are ahead of their time, and suffer for it."

"You are right," my husband replied, "but are you so sure that we are ahead of our time?"

My Sons' Heavenly Kingdom
Yesterday I visited my husband's grave. Both my sons came with me. They asked me if I knew where their father was now. "In the realm of the spirits of the dead, according to the Jewish view," I answered. "And according to the Babylonians?" they asked.

"According to the Babylonians, he is also in the realm of the dead. In the Babylonian view, it is the responsibility of the sons to pour water on their father's grave so that in the grave the father does not suffer from thirst. If he is fortunate and strong enough he will swim across the river of death and reach the Island of the Blessed. To date only two people have succeeded, as far as we know: Ut-Napishtim and his wife, and of course Ishtar, but she is a goddess."[54]

"Mother," they said, "you know how father often told us about Ezekiel's vision of the resurrection. There is one nation which knows more about life after death than the Jews and the Babylonians together, and they are our new overlords, the Persians. Their virtue and tolerance are displayed again in their knowledge of death. They tell us that after death the immortal part of man, the soul, is freed from the body and is borne over the shining Cinvat bridge, the bridge of winds, up to the heights of Elburz, to the borders of heaven. It's Sraosha who leads them there. The souls are then weighed on heavenly scales which do not favor anybody by a hair's breadth. Lords and kings are judged the same as the poorest man. The good deeds are set against the evil deeds, and if the good deeds weigh heavier than the evil deeds, and that is definitely the case with our father, the soul gets the chance to do penance for the evil deeds and enter eternal life."[55]

"Oh, boys!" I exclaimed. "You are making up some fantastic tales!"

"They are not fantastic," they retorted, their cheeks pink with excitement. "Look here, mother. Not only individual lives, but the whole history of the world is seen by the Persians as a struggle between good and evil. It is entirely different with the Jews who even want to make us believe that Satan has access to heaven and is allowed to accuse the righteous.[56] It is much more in line with the old Hebrew prophets who spoke of 'The day of the Lord.'[57] According to the Persian version there is an end to history and then there will be a judgment. All evil, all suffering, all injustice will be condemned and wiped out; then the world will be entirely purified and there will be new life and eternal life in heavenly perfection."

I knew of course that my sons had studied Persian literature and religion. I did not know, however, that it had such an appeal for them. I understood why the visitor from Isaiah's school who had come to see us a long time ago could also speak of the advent of a kingdom of righteousness. Had he learned that from the Persians? But the difficulty is still to find out who belongs to the righteous and who belongs to the unrighteous.

I turned to my sons and asked them: "Is this the new life that Ezekiel spoke of? Or is Yahweh, as your father once said, only to be experienced beyond our experience?'"

COMMENTARY AND NOTES

I. On "Conflict in Corinth": I Corinthians 12—14
The Theological Dictionary of the New Testament, the lexi-
con "Die Religion in Geschichte und Gegenwart," form-
and redaction-critical research, and those theologians
who have made us reflect fundamentally on the task of the
translation of a biblical text from the shore of the first
centuries of our era in a Hellenistic milieu to the shore of
our own time—all this has forced us to take a careful look
at the biblical vocabulary and its complex significance,
including the meanings behind the words. It is in the
context of this enormous research that the great critical
commentaries to the biblical books and the theologies of
the New and Old Testament were written. The springtime
of exegesis was also the autumn of systematic theology.
The exegetes have not made the task of the systematic and
practical theologians easier. Some of them have said
explicitly that it is their job to make life more difficult for
the systematicians. If we are, however, of the opinion that
this is only one and by no means the only task of exegetical
research, then we might reasonably expect some help for
the exegesis, the interpretation of our own time from the
exegetes of biblical texts. How the cultural and theological
pluralism of biblical concepts and myths is relevant (or not
relevant) for us today is a question that cannot be avoided.
  Whether my "narrative exegesis" makes the task of

the systematicians easier or not, I cannot judge. But I hope that it introduces the critical interpretation of the Bible to the whole people of God, which—in my opinion—should be the sphere for theological reflection par excellence. In the final analysis it is the people of God (which also includes the theologians) who are responsible for theology. Today, however, those members of the people of God who can think theologically and want to enter into that critical process, which in my opinion is necessary for the understanding of the Bible, are denied their theological responsibility simply because their culture does not include the tools of classical critical exegesis. In order to place theology where it belongs, right in the middle of the people of God, the different exegetical options must be made visible. They become visible when placed in their *social* and *cultural* context and, to use a sweeping expression, not merely in their semantic context. The social and cultural incarnation of theology must become visible. The articulation of the theological "Ueberbau" is not sufficient on its own; it is just as important that the social tensions between Erastus and Chloe, between Stephanas and Tertius be made visible.

It is well known that the writings of Paul are not merely theological documents, if in fact such a thing exists at all. His theological ideas are inseparable from the so-called non-theological traditions and concepts of his culture. That in fact is the case in all theological struggles from Marcion to the Reformation and Northern Ireland. They always have been at one and the same time theological, political and cultural struggles.

A narrative exegesis therefore does not divorce the theological element from its cultural and social base, but has to argue its theology in its involvement, in its function, in these other fields of conflict. That also does not mean that the theological struggle now has to be reduced to its political and social projections as is sometimes the case in the interpretations of sociologists of religion. It is much more important that the multi-dimensional and multi-colored structure of the texts be revealed.

The multi-dimensional structure of narrative exegesis has its advantages and disadvantages. One advantage is that in a story several persons can argue with each other, thus bringing several points of view simultaneously into interplay. Different readers will identify with the points of view of the biblical author or of the interpreter. By introducing not only the author but also the recipients of Paul's letter, a part of the early history of its reception is brought into the exegesis.

It is quite clear that with this method the varieties of interpretation of a text still remain restricted. They are restricted by the dimensions, the colors introduced into the story, in other words, by the points of view which the exegete introduces into the story through the characters of the story. They are restricted by the overtones and undertones of the specific key in which the narrator has chosen to tell his story. Within this choice different readers will hear different overtones and undertones, not any number, but as many as the chosen tonality contains.

This advantage of narrative exegesis is also its disadvantage. It is not unambigously clear from which point of view the exegete argues, which points of view he considers to be appropriate or inappropriate, which of the overtones in the chosen tonality he would like to emphasize and which he would prefer to play down. One can therefore accuse this exegesis of being inexact. This lack of precision is the price to be paid for the communication of biblical exegesis to a readership or an audience of mixed cultural and educational background. But the unambiguity of an exegesis which argues from one and only one point of view has equal disadvantages. The most important disadvantage is this: If the reader or listener is neither able nor willing to accept the point of view of the exegete because it is too high, too low or too far removed from his own, he is then unable to understand anything at all that the exegete wants to communicate. Another fact is connected with these advantages and disadvantages. An exegesis which is structured like a chain of arguments is as strong as its weakest link. If one link breaks (because it is too weak or because that particular argument is not understood), then the whole argument collapses. The chain does not break only in one link, but it falls apart. On the other hand a narrative exegesis is like a rope, the intertwining of numerous strands. If one strand breaks the rope does not break. That is why it is possible to follow a story without necessarily understanding every single detail in it. This is not the case for a chain of arguments.

This is neither a case against exegesis as a chain of arguments nor a plea for narrative exegesis. I am only trying to analyze their respective advantages and disadvantages. That we need both methods in theology and in the Church is clear to me. But as we have little experience and practice in narrative exegesis and as this form of exegesis is vital for a dialogue with Christians from the third world (and in fact the whole people of God), I think it is a good thing to practice this other kind of theology. My main aim in this is not merely to assist preachers and teachers in their everyday work, but rather to develop a method of theology which does not give up its commitment to critical exegesis while using the mode of narration. If such exegesis in dialogue with the whole people of God and with third world Christians is to be of any value, it cannot be any less scholarly than other forms of exegesis. The critical element of exegesis and theology must not be sacrificed.

The two narrative exegeses in this book are a test for the applicability of this method. The test is passed when illiterate Christians and academic theologians alike can understand it and see its relevance. For a further development of this argument see my essay on "The Other Exegesis" in *Horizons in Biblical Theology* (Vol. III, 1981, Pittsburgh Theological Seminary), in *Erfahrungen der Leibhaftigkeit, Interkulturelle Theologie I* and *Umgang mit Mythen, Interkulturelle Theologie II* (Munich, Kaiser, 1979/82).

For the background research of *Conflict in Corinth* two essays have been of particular importance: Gerd Theissen, "Soziale Schichtung in der korinthischen Gemeinde. Ein Beitrag zur Soziologie des hellenistischen Urchristentums" (*ZNW* 65, 1974, 232-272 = Theissen, *Studien zur Soziologie des Urchristentums* (WUNT 19), Tubingen, Mohr, 1979, 231-271), and Dieter Luhrmann, "Wo man nicht mehr Sklave oder Freier ist. Ueberlegungen zur Struktur fruhchristlicher Gemeinden" (in: *Wort und Dienst*. Jahrbuch der Kirchl. Hochschule Bethel, NF 13, 1975, 53-84).

In these two essays the following literature is discussed: S. S. Bartchy, *Mallon chresai*. First-Century Slavery and the Interpretation of I Corinthians 7:21, SBL Dissertation Series, 1973; H. Bellen, *Studien zur Sklavenflucht im romischen Kaiserreich*, 1971; H. Bolkestein, *Wohltatigkeit und Armenpflege im vorchristlichen Altertum*, Utrecht 1939 = Groningen 1967; F. Bomer, *Untersuchungen uber die Religion der Sklaven in Griechenland und Rom*, 4 Vols, AaMz 1957-1963; G. Bornkamm, "Herrenmahl und Kirche bei Paulus," *ZThK* 53, 1956, 312ff. (= Studien zu Antike und Christentum, Ges. Aufsatze II, 1963, 138-176); P. R. Coleman-Norton, "The Apostle Paul and the Roman Law of Slavery," in *Studies in Roman Economic and Social History*, Festschr. A. C. Johnson, 1951, 155-177; J. E. Crouch, *The Origin and Intention of the Colossian Haustafel*, FRLANT 109, 1972, 172f.; A. Deissman, *Light from the Ancient East* (ET 1910, rev. 1927, repr. 1978); M. I. Finley (ed.), *Slavery in Classical Antiquity*, 1960; D. Georgi, *Die Gegner des Paulus im 2. Korintherbrief*. Studien zur religiosen Propaganda in der Spatantike, WMANT 11, 1964; M. Greeven, *Das Hauptproblem der Sozialethik in der neueren Stoa und im Urchristentum*, 1935, 28-61; H. Gulzow, *Christentum und Sklaverei in den ersten drei Jahrhunderten*, 1969; E. A. Judge, *Christliche Gruppen in nichtchristlicher Gesellschaft*, 1964; F. Kiechle, *Sklavenarbeit und technischer Fortschritt im romischen Reich*, Forschungen zur antiken Sklaverei, Vol. 3, 1971; H. Kreissig, "Zur sozialen Zusammensetzung der fruhchristlichen Gemeinden im ersten Jahrhundert u.Z.," *Eirene* 6, 1967, 91-100; G. Kretschmar, "Ein Beitrag zur Frage nach dem Ursprung fruhchristlicher Askese," *ZThK* 61, 1964, 27-64; D. Schroeder, *Die Haustafeln des Neuen Testaments*, theol. diss. Hamburg (typescript), 1969; S. Schulz, "Hat Christus die Sklaven befreit?" *EvKomm* 5, 1972, 13-17; E. Troeltsch, *Die Soziallehren der christlichen Kirchen und Gruppen*, chapter 1, Ges. Schr. 1 (1919), 15-178; J. Vogt, *Sklaverei und Humanitat*, Historia Einzelschrift 8, 1972[2]; W. L. Westermann, *The Slave Systems of Greek and Roman Antiquity*, 1960; U. Wilcken, *Griechische Ostraka aus Aegypten und Nubien. Ein Beitrag zur antiken Wirtschaftsgeschichte*, Vol. I, Munich = Amsterdam 1970. Ample bibliography in my essay "The Other Exegesis" and in H. C. Kee, *Christian Origins in Sociological Perspective,* 1980.

I used the following commentaries: H. Conzelmann, *Der erste Brief an die Korinther* (Gottingen, Meyer K V); D. Wendlnd, *Die Briefe an die Korinther* (Gottingen 1963, NTD 7); F. Godet, *Commentaire sur la premiere epitre aux Corinthiens* (1885 = Neuchatel 1965, 2 vols, also English); J. C. Hurd, *The Origin of I Corinthians*, 1965.

For phenomena similar but not identical to Corinthian Christianity in today's Christianity see my *The Charismatic and Pentecostal Movements* (Minneapolis, Minn., 1976[2]); *Die Pfingstkirchen. Selbstdarstellungen, Dokumente, Kommentare* (Stuttgart 1971); *Pentecost Between*

Black and White. Five case studies on Pentecost and Politics (Belfast 1974). Abbreviations according to RGG³ and TRE.

Notes

1. G. Theissen, "Soziale Schichtung," 263: J. A. D. Larsen, "Roman Greece," in: *An Economic Survey of Ancient Rome* IV, ed. T. Frank, Baltimore 1938, 259-498, 472. Plutarch (mor. 831 A).

2. To be exact between 7 B.C. and 3 A.D. (G. Theissen, "Soziale Schichtung," 263); our story suggests the latter date.

3. Rom. 16:22.

4. Acts 18; E. Haenchen, *Die Apostelgeschichte,* Gottingen 1959¹² (Meyer K III), 478

5. Acts 18:7; Haenchen, 476; Theissen, 252.

6. Luhrmann (Wo man nicht mehr Sklave oder Freier ist, 55f.) estimates that "about ten percent of the population of the Imperium Romanum" were associated with the Jewish synagogue. Cp A. v. Harnack, *Die Mission des Christentums in den ersten drei Jahrhunderten,* 1924⁴, 13 (about V. Tcherikover, *Hellenistic Civilization and the Jews,* 1966³, 292-295 (cautious, with the result 294f.: "It is at any rate clear that the Jewish population was quite considerable in the Graeco-Roman world, especially in the eastern half of the Mediterranean"); H. Hegermann, "Das hellenistische Judentum," in: *Umwelt des Urchristentums* I, 1967², 292-345 (294: "at least a tenth of all inhabitants"); literature discussed in Luhrmann.

7. Rom. 16:23; I Cor. 1:14; Theissen, 251.

8. Rom. 16:23; on   Erastus in detail Theissen, 237-246; J. Cadbury, Erastus of Corinth," *JBL* 50, 1931, 42-58; P. Landvogt, *Epigraphische Untersuchungen uber den oikonomos. Ein Beitrag zum hellenistischen Beamtenwesen.* Diss. Strasbourg 1908.

9. Acts 18:8; I Cor. 1:14; Haenchen, 472; Theissen, 236f (lit.).

10. I Cor. 16:22; Conzelmann, *Korintherbrief,* 360.

11. I Cor. 11:23-26.

12. I Cor. 1:11; this interpretation of "hoi Chloes" is based on Theissen, 255, who describes them as "representatives of the lower strata of society." According to Theissen the formula "hoi

Chloes" excludes relatives and sons "almost certainly."

13. Rom. 16:23. Theissen (237-241) discusses in detail the translation and function of an "oikonomos tes poleos."

14. I Cor. 11:23-26.

15. I Cor. 12:12f.

16. Rom. 16:1.

17. I Cor. 12:14-20.

18. Livius II 32; Plato, State, 46c-d; Josephus, Bell.Jud. 4/VIII/406; Conzelmann, 248; A. Bittlinger, *Gifts and Graces*. A commentary on I Corinthians 12—14 (London 1967), 54ff.

19. I Cor. 12:21-24.

20. Cp. the reconstruction by Kent of an Erastus inscription "(praenomen nomen) Erastus pro aedilit (at) e s(ua) p(ecunia) stravit" (Erastus paid for the laying of this pavement out of his own pocket in recognition of his election to the office of an aedil). J. K. Kent, *The Inscriptions 1926-1950. Corinth. Results of Excavations* VIII, 3. Princeton 1966, 18-19, no. 232. Discussion of the literature in Theissen, 242.

21. I Cor. 12:24f.

22. I Cor. 12:26.

23. 2 Cor. 10:10.

24. "Ekklesia is the designation not of any one private cultic association or religious society which one could choose to join. For that there were other terms available in the Hellenistic time such as thiasos (cultic society), eranos (association for cultic meals), koinon (fellowship), synodos (meeting), etc. Ekklesia is the designation of a people—to be exact, of the citizens' meeting of God...." (A. Rich, *Glaube in politischer Entscheidung*, Zurich 1962, 39f.). The secular texts in K. L. Schmidt, art. "ekklesia", *TDNT* III, 514f.

25. Plato, Resp. 364f.; E. Rohde, *Seelenkult und Unsterblichkeit der Griechen* II, 1921[8], 128, note 5 (inscription in: *Jahreshefte des Oesterr. Archaol. Instituss* Wien 23, 1926, Beibl. 23f.); A. Oepke, art. "baptizo," *TDNT* I, 542; H. Conzelmann, *Korintherbrief*, 327. I Cor 15:29.

26. Eph. 5:14; an old baptismal hymn; cp. M. Dibelius, *An die Kolosser, Epheser, an Philemon* (Gottingen 1953[3] HNT 12), 90f. H. Schlier, *Der Brief an die Epheser* Dusseldorf 1957) 240ff.

27. I Cor. 16:17.

28. Rom. 16:23

29. Gal. 3:27.

30. I Cor. 12:3. W. Schmithals, *Die Gnosis in Korinth. Eine Untersuchung zu den Korintherbriefen* (Gottingen 1956) aruges on the basis of this passage that there were people in Corinth for whom "kyrios Christos" and "anathema Iesous" were no contradiction. They said "hoti Iesous ouk estin ho Christos" (1 Jn. 2:22) (45ff.), a thesis which is rejected by Conzelmann (241f.); see also Hurd, 102, note 2, and 193.

31. I Cor. 13:1.

32. I Cor. 13:2.

33. I Cor. 13:3.

34. I Cor. 13:4-7.

35. Many contemporary parallels in Conzelmann, 257ff.

36. I Cor. 13:8-10.

37. I Cor. 13:11-12.

38. I Cor. 13:13.

39. I Cor. 14:16. That the "idiotai" were seated on special seats is a suggestion by Conzelmann (282).

40. I Cor. 12:24.

41. Rom. 16:21.

42. I Cor. 14:33-35.

43. "This part (14:33b-36) which is in itself consistent disrupts the argument: The topic of prophecy is interrupted; the ductus of the argument is spoiled. Its content is in contradiction to 11:2ff., where the public ministry of women in the church is presupposed. This contradiction remains even if one ascribes chapters 11 and 14 to different letters. One has to add to this particularities of style and thought. Finally verse 37 does not link up with verse 36, but with verse 33a. The passage has to be considered an interpolation. The not very lucid verse 36 is meant to emphasize the 'ecumenical' validity of the interpolation. But it only mirrors the bourgeois stabilization of the church at about the time of the pastoral letters: one accepts the universal custom. Whoever defends the text as original has to take refuge in unreliable thought constructions" (Conzelman, 289f.; cp. also Else Kahler, *Kie Frau in den paulinischen Briefen*, Zurich 1960).

44. I Cor. 13:7.

45. I Cor. 13:6.

46. I Cor. 14:15-17.
47. I Cor. 14:18-20.
48. W. J. Hollenweger, *Pentecost Between Black and White.*
49. I Cor. 14:24-25.
50. I Cor. 13:13.
51. I Cor. 14:29.
52. I Cor. 14:30.
53. I Cor. 14:31-33.
54. Rom. 16:22 ("Perhaps 'en kyrio' means that he wrote it free of charge for Paul": Theissen, 255).

II. On "Memoirs of an Old Man": Ezekiel 37

The theological problem which is dealt with in "Memoirs of an Old Man" is as follows: How does one deal with a promise which has not been fulfilled? Possible solutions are:

- It has not been fulfilled yet, but it will be later, perhaps being fulfilled in a way different from the original expectation.
- The fulfillment of the promise will take place in the next world.
- The promise was false; it will never be fulfilled.
- It is part of the nature of faith that one has to live with unfulfilled promises.

Behind the question about unfulfilled promises lies the basic question about how faith is experienced (cp. H. H. Schmid, *Altorientalische Welt in der alttestamentlichen Theologie*, Zurich 1974, especially pp. 26-30, 109-120, 160-164.

Unlike a theological essay, in a narrative exegesis no dogmatic statements can be explicitly expressed, not even the author's convictions. However, the dramatis personae can make dogmatic statements and argue for their convictions. As is usual in a drama these statements will be contradicted, or at least relativized, by statements from other characters. This method, it seems to me, fits the findings of exegetical scholarship which teaches us that the

Bible, and especially the Old Testament, rarely contains uncontested statements. He who holds the Bible to be a foundation book of the Christian faith—and I am of this opinion—has to wrestle with the fact that already in the Bible the search for the truth and the articulation of faith appears as an ongoing process. However, the visible part of this process is a starting point for the discovery of the truth, but only a starting point. It points us in the right direction. In particular the statements of the priestly writer, of the prophet Ezekiel, of the psalmists, of Deutero- and Trito-Isaiah, of Jeremiah and of the other theological authors mentioned in the narrative exegesis were contested in their time and sometimes later. The open-ended conclusion of the exegesis fits well this questionability and questioning of one biblical author by other biblical authors.

As in the first narrative, here too theology is placed in its context in social, cultural and political conflicts. I do not need to repeat what was said on this in relation to "Conflict in Corinth." However, one has to give greater attention to the discussion of tradition when we interpret Old Testament texts. That is perhaps the reason for the choice of a greater span of time in the story.

I must thank Professor H. H. Schmid of Zurich for important advice and information on technical points. Any possible mistakes are mine.

I found the following background literature useful: Martin Noth, *History of Israel* (German: 1954[2]; English: 1958); W. Zimmerli, *Ezechiel* (Neukirchen 1969, 2 vols., BK XIII/1-2); H. von Glasenapp, *Die nichtchristlichen Religion*, 1957 (Fischer-Lekion 1); S. Moscati, *Geschichte und Kultur der semitischen Volker* (Zurich 1953, Italian 1949; German: Urban Bucherei); R. Bach, art. Exil, RGG[3], II, 817-19; W. Zimmerli, Art. Ezechiel und Ezechielbuch, RGG[3], II, 844-850; G. v. Rad, *Old Testament Theology* (German 1965[3]; English: 1962, 165).

Notes

1. 605 B.C.
2. Jer. 46:10; W. Rudolph, *Jeremiah* (Tubingen 1958, HAT 12), 248.
3. 2 Kgs. 24.
4. Ez. 3:15; W. Zimmerli, *Ezekiel* I, 83.
5. Martin Noth, *History of Israel*, 293; *The Babylonian Expedition of the University of Pennsylvania*, Ser. A, Cuneiform Texts ed. by H. V. Hilprecht, Vol. IX.X; *The University of Pennsylvania. The Museum. Publications of the Babylonian Section*, Vol. II; G. Gardascia, *Les archives de Murasu, une famille d'hommes d'affaires babyloniens a l'epoque perse*, 1951; W. Zimmerli, *Ezechiel I*, 40. Murashu & Sons Ltd. is first documented in Persian times.
6. Jer. 29:5f.
7. Ez. 14:1; 20:1: "elders."
8. M. Noth, *History of Israel*, 295; Ez. 1:1, 1:3; 3:15; 3:23; 10:15; 10:22; 43:3; G. v. Rad, *Old Testament Theology* II, 223; W. Zimmerli, *Ezechiel* I, 39.
9. Ez. 3:3.
10. Ez. 4.
11. Ps. 137; cp. H.-J. Kraus, *Psalmen* II (Neukirchen 1961, BK XV/2). I have changed the text into the present tense.
12. Ez. 29:7; Is. 36:6.
13. W. Zimmerli, *Ezechiel* I, 43.
14. On creation and the priestly writer, I used H.-H. Schmid, *Die Steine und das Wort. Fug und Unfug biblischer Archaologie* (Zurich 1975); W. H. Schmidt, *Die Schopfungsgeschichte der Priesterschrift* (Neukirchen 1964 WMANT 17),. esp. 87; C. Westermann, *Genesis I* (Neukirchen 1974, BK 1/1), esp. 146 and 242f.: (a) P does not wish to make his own understanding of the process of creation absolute, and thereby declare all other explanations to be false. If he takes up older representations and lets them speak in his report, we too have the freedom, on the basis of P's fundamental openness, to continue our research into the beginnings of the world. (b) The tendency of the creation report of P is to guard the secret of creation; he in no way gives a representation which provides ready answers to all our questions about creation, but instead he deliberately leaves his

listeners without answers in many places. (c) For P there is not yet a conflict between scientific and theological explanations for the origin of the world and man. The same is equally valid concerning the common tradition behind him. The demythologizing tendency in P has the effect that the gods are removed from heaven and earth ('Weltall, Himmel und Erde werden radikal entgottert'). Heaven and earth are thereby accessible to human research and questioning, in that every mythical-divine character is denied to them. P points in the direction of scientific thinking by introducing definitions and categories, by reducing stars to their bare function, by understanding the origin of plants and animals as species and finally by seeing the origin of the world in time phases" (*op. cit.*, 242f.). The only question here is whether there is a conflict between (a) and (b) on the one hand and (c) on the other—if not in P, at least in his audience.

15. W. H. Schmidt, *op. cit.*, 119. S. Aalen, art. 'or, TWBAT I, 171. I hope that my presentation of the stars as naked lights does not fall into the trap of the caricature criticized by Westermann (*Genesis I*, 179).

16. Jer. 29.

17. Ez. 33:32.

18. Ez. 37:11. According to W. Zimmerli (*Ezechiel II*, 890) "the origin of the prophet's whole picture obviously lies in the word that he, the prophet, according to 37:11, repeats *from the mouth of the people.*"

19. Ez. 18:2; Jer. 31:29; Num. 14:18; W. Zimmerli, *Ezechiel I*, 103.

20. Ez. 4:13.

21. G. v. Rad, *Old Testament Theology* II, 272; W. Zimmerli, *Ezechiel I*, 98ff.

22. Ez. 37:11.

23. Ez. 37.

24. Ez. 17:2.

25. Ez. 37:11-14 (a lter interpretation?).

26. Is. 46:13; 51:5; 52:10; on the entire Deutero-isaiah passage cp. von Rad, *Old Testament Theology*, II, 273f.

27. Is. 45:2f.

28. Is. 48:14; 45:13.

29. Is. 45:1.

30. Is. 40.
31. Is. 49:11.
32. Is. 49:10, 42:16.
33. Is. 49:13; 55:12.
34. Is. 42:17; 45:24.
35. Is. 49:7.
36. Is. 54:7, 10.
37. Is. 42:14.
38. Is. 50:1.
39. M. Noth, *History of Israel*, 300.
40. Ezra 6:3-5; M. Noth, *History of Israel*, 305f.
41. Ezra 5:14-16; M. Noth, *op. cit.*, 308.

42. Hag. 1:2f. Haggai must be placed some years later in the history of Israel than, for dramatic reasons, he is placed here.

43. Hag. 1:9f.

44. Neh. 13:23-25. Nehemiah is to be dated later. In the interest of the narrative, the episode is brought forward.

45. Jer. 29:6; but did Jeremiah mean the letter to be taken in the way Seraiah understood it?

46. Is. 59:1-4; G. v. Rad, *Old Testament Theology* II, 280.

47. Is. 59:8-11.

48. Is. 60.

49. O. Eissfeldt, art. Astarte, RGG[3] I, 661; Eissfeldt, art. Aschera, RGG[3] I, 637; J. C. de Moor, art. Aschera, TWBAT I, 473-481.

50. Jer. 44 and W. Rudolph, *Jeremiah*, 239ff. Re the worship of the goddess Anath (O. Eissfeldt, Anath, RGG[3] I, 356) in Elephantine, see M. Noth, *History of Israel*, 293. Edition of the texts and English translation of the Elephantine papyrii by A. E. Cowley, *Aramaic Papyrii of the Fifth Century B.C.*, 1923.

51. Friedrich Jeremias, "Semitische Volker in Vorderasien," in A. Bertholet/E. Lehmann (eds.), *Lehrbuch der Religionsgeschichte*, begrundet von Chantepie de la Saussaye (Tubingen 1925[4]), esp. I, 552ff; G. v. Rad, *Old Testament Theology* I, 85.

52. G. v. Rad, *op. cit.* I, 28.

53. Is. 66:13.

54. F. Jeremias, *op. cit.*, 585ff.

55. E. Lehmann, "Die Perser," in A. Bertholet/E. Lehmann (eds.), *op. cit.*, II, esp. 248ff.

56. Job 1:6, 2:1.

57. Is. 2:12; 13:6; Ez. 30:3; Amos 5:18; 5:20; H. W. Wolff, *Dodekapropheton 2, Joel und Amos* (Neukirchen 1969, BK XIV/2), 38f., 298-302; H. Wildberger, *Jesaja* (Neukirchen 1972, BK X/1) I, 105f, 108f, II, 516f.; W. Zimmerli, *Ezechiel* I, 166-168, II, 728-40.